James Edgecombe lives with his wife, Yuko, and their two children, Rintaro and Hinako, on the edge of Dartmoor National Park in southwest Devon. Having lived and taught in Hokkaido, Japan, he now teaches at Tavistock College, while also pursuing his PhD in creative writing at Plymouth University, where he is assistant editor of *Short Fiction: the Visual Literary Journal*. The tension between the visual and written arts has long fascinated him.

The Art of Kozu is a stunningly well-controlled piece of writing. Startlingly ambitious in its geographic and temporal range and in its subject matter, the writing makes remarkable use of voice and deployment of detail.

This work deals with art, death, aging, beauty, race, war and memory – and it's a testament to the skill of its writer that after finishing it, I immediately read it again.

The novella was absolutely a stand-out piece, memorable, difficult, haunting and intelligent – never underestimating the reader and demonstrating with absolute clarity that a shorter work can have the thematic and emotional complexity of a full length novel.

Jenn Ashworth
Chair of the Judging Panel

THE ART OF KOZU

James Edgecombe

SANDSTONEPRESS
HIGHLAND | SCOTLAND

First published in Great Britain
and the United States of America in 2014
Sandstone Press Ltd
PO Box 5725
One High Street
Dingwall
Ross-shire
IV15 9WJ
Scotland.

www.sandstonepress.com

Editor: Robert Davidson

The Art of Kozu is the winner of the inaugural MMU Novella
Award, a partnership between Manchester Metropolitan
University's Cheshire Campus, Sandstone Press and Time to Read,
a forum of 22 library authorities in the North West of England.

The publisher acknowledges support from Creative Scotland
towards publication of this volume.

ISBN: 978-1-910124-00-0
ISBNe: 978-1-910124-01-7

Cover design by Mark Ecob
Typesetting by Iolaire Typesetting, Newtonmore
Printed and bound by Totem, Poland

My thanks to Anthony Caleshu, Aya Louise McDonald, Gerard Donovan, Tom Vowler, Tom D'Evelyn, Madeleine Findlay; my mother and father, Carol and Colin Edgecombe; my children, Rintaro and Hinako, and, above all, Yuko Edgecombe.

To my children.

'Messrs. O'Brien & Sons:

Gentlemen . . . At present and for some time past I see no reason why I should paint any pictures.

P.S. I will paint for money at any time. Any subject, any size.'

Winslow Homer (1836–1910)

YUICHIRO KOZU
(1878–1953)

A RETROSPECTIVE

Born in 1878, the first son of military surgeon Roan
Kozu (1855–1919), Yuichiro Kozu grew up in the port
city of Hakodate, on the southern tip of the Kameda
Peninsula, Hokkaido, Japan's great island-wilderness
and one of the country's first international ports.* The
city, however, was fortified; the site of the last stand of
the Tokugawan rebels during the Boshin War (1868-
1869) and an important outpost built by an empire
ever weary of its neighbour, Russia. It is little wonder
then, bearing these facts in mind, that Hakodate sig-
nificantly influenced Kozu's development as an artist:
it symbolised for him what it meant to be 'Japanese on

---

* The other ports were Yokohama (Honshu) and Nagasaki (Kyushu),
which were opened up to trade with the West, after Commodore
Perry forced the Tokugawa Shogunate to sign the Kanagawa Treaty
in 1854, thus ending *Sakoku*, the Age of Isolation.

the edge of the world,' to belong to a nation looking outward, if guardedly so.

In 1906, he went to Paris. There, he refused to attend any of the 'anesthetising academies' crowded with his contemporaries, often quoting Monet's instructions to Renoir, Sisley and Bazille: 'We must leave this studio and our teacher. The air is unwholesome. Where is the sincerity?' Having travelled half-way around the world, Kozu looked homeward, to *the Japanese* genre of the bijinga, those portraits of beautiful Japanese women that made him so famous in the 1920s (at the time he even outsold Picasso).

Kozu showed ambivalence towards the Japanese art world, staunchly dismissing a num*ber* of h*is country-*men as omu, or parrots. To him, his contemporaries seemed hell-bent on copying the methods and innovations of the west, without first allowing foreign ideas to percolate through and be absorbed by the Japanese sensibility. If a Japanese artist were to produce meaningful works, he said, they first had to plumb the depths of western oil paints, that gap between their realism and the uniqueness of the Japanese body. For Kozu, the artist's ultimate goal was clear: to illuminate the Yamato spirit.

After the declaration of 'Total War' against China in 1937, and the reorganisation of the Japanese government's official salons, Kozu became a war artist for the Imperial Army. For this reason his reputation suffered in the post-war period.

Only recently has academic interest in Kozu's paintings revived. Such tentative explorations have borne interesting fruit. Prominent critic, Daichi Ando has asked that we, 'look past the cruelty depicted in Kozu's war art, to dig deep into the plight of those civilians trapped on the outlying islands of the empire, or the charred remains of our troops left on the field of battle in Mongolia, and to see the horror, made clear through Kozu's canvases, for what it is: a lament.'* The artist's sympathy and pity for those individuals he depicted is never in doubt.

Kozu died in Nice, France, in 1953.

Kasumi Takayanagi, 2014
Director of the Shin Midori Gallery, Ginza, Tokyo

---

* Sadly, few of these paintings exist today: most were destroyed in the firebombing of Tokyo, in March 1945.

PART I

SELLING YUMIKO

The Ginza, Tokyo, 1927

Ryunosuke Akutagawa, a friend of mine, and great writer according to his obituaries, committed suicide six months ago. I didn't know him as a master of words – he was always so quiet. I never read anything he wrote. I only mention him because he hated any painting by Kozu. Often, we would argue over Kozu's virtues as a human being, his vices as an artist of the real, for hours in the backroom after I had shut up for the night.

Since his early twenties, Akutagawa would come to my gallery to gaze at the oils on display. I saw a melancholy in him even then, when he was still a student. I thought that showing him the canvases I brought back from Europe, the monstrosities I bought straight from their Parisian artists, would lighten his mood. 'See how ugly they are?' I used to say to him, 'you wouldn't find anything as detestable as these on sale in the Mitsukoshi Department Store!' I told him the reason I spent so much money on canvases I didn't like, all portraits of some type or the other, was so that they could never be exhibited in Europe as visions of Japanese beauty.

A week before he murdered himself, Akutagawa came by the gallery and said, 'I need to see the Kozu portrait!' He claimed to have finally understood his lifelong melancholy that morning, after a night wandering around Honjo, where he saw a horse tethered to a cart beneath an iron bridge. The thick purple patches of shadow in the structure's metalwork, around its rivets, across the horse's back, around the cloud of steam puffed into the air by the beast, its great form little more than a silhouette in the morning twilight, struck him with the force of *déjà vu*. He knew the street before him, the bridge over his head, had walked that same route as a child. But that morning, it was fresh to his eyes, like a painting by one of his favourites, Van Gogh.

He told me he needed to know if the Kozu portrait could reproduce in him that same sadness. To him the Kozu was a step backward from the avant-garde, rendered by an artist who did not understand the expressive power of colour. To such an artist as Kozu, he would say, the muddy vulgarity of detail was prized above all else.

The reason I mention this is because your wife has shown a keen interest in the painting to which I am referring. That is why I must ask you whether she wants this painting for the right reasons. It has a history – a story I will tell you, just as I told my writer friend that morning when he came to the gallery, faint from the summer heat.

But it requires us to sit. At least for a little while. Here in this corner, where we can enjoy the morning light.

The cat in the foreground, its fur exquisitely rendered in *sumi* ink, stroke by stroke, hair by hair, may offer a brilliant contrast to the oils of the female figure, but it is only an adornment. Yuichiro Kozu was admittedly good at painting cats. But when it came to women, he was a genius. If I thought someone was to take ownership of this piece simply because they thought the cat charming, I would fear the ghost of Akutagawa for the rest of my days. Be assured, Yuichiro Kozu only included the beast to demonstrate his skill at rendering the texture of its fur. With the woman's skin as clear as it is, pure like porcelain, her pubic hair covered by her hand, there was no other chance to bring to life the rough tactility of common objects. Even her hair is as smooth as the ribbon that fastens her braid.

Maybe the cat is as good a place to start as any. He was called Hugo. Yuichiro bought him in anticipation of his brother's arrival in Paris. Jun Kozu hated cats. It was the summer of 1911, just before the theft of the

Mona Lisa from the Louvre that August. Paris was already hot, I remember that much.

Jun's hatred of cats can partially explain Yuichiro's interest in portraiture from a young age. Let suffice, Jun had demonstrated to his older brother the benefits of *shasei*, of sketching from life, when they were little more than children. Jun was the hands on type, while Yuichiro, at first at least, was the visionary. Jun, long before he left Hakodate for medical school in Tokyo, used to perform his own anatomical studies on the neighbourhood strays. Yuichiro would join him, sketching the dissections, so that he came to see and understand the internal workings of pregnancy, death, how bones were held in place, how their nuances dictated the topography of what lay above, the musculature of the body, the contours of the skin. Just like the legend of the Heian artist Yoshide, who could paint people with lifelike precision, as long as he had seen them with his own eyes, Yuichiro could paint any cat, no matter how contorted its pose.

His ability to paint cats was a skill he put to good use in Paris. That was how he met the girl in the painting, his model, Yumiko, the young wife of one of his rivals. You see, Yuichiro loved women. When searching out new lovers on the Metro, he would drop his newspaper on the lap of some pretty girl and, as she picked it up, he would say, 'What a coincidence, I see you read *L'Anarchie*, too! My name is Yuichiro Kozu. I paint cats.'

According to Yuichiro, the sight of Yumiko's face amongst all those Parisians on the Line 6 train was like spotting a wild cherry in blossom on a mountainside. The symbolism of the radical newspaper in her hands must have meant little to her, caused no shock, or excitement because when he asked her what she was doing on the train, she replied that she liked to travel around Paris by Metro. She didn't care if her husband owned an automobile. Yuichiro explained her love of trains like this: although she was raised in view of a great naval base in Tokyo, the Metro instilled within her such a sense of modernity that she felt compelled to use it on her daily trips north from Montparnasse to the Louvre, the more circuitous route the better.

Yuichiro asked her to model for him then and there, before all those people in the carriage. He enjoyed talking about such things, whether business or personal, in front of the foreigners in that brazen way, enjoying the freedom that comes when one knows his language is a room without windows. According to Yuichiro, she agreed without hesitation.

A month later, Yumiko laid herself over the Line 6 track at the Passy Station, the very same line she had been riding north on when Yuichiro introduced himself. I can remember the day after that incident. I was eating breakfast with both Yuichiro and Jun outside the Café Houdini in Montparnasse.

'She leaned over the track, as the train moved off,' Yuichiro said.

It seemed odd that the couple drinking coffee next to us could smile and hold hands as Yuichiro read the news aloud, translating the story straight from the paper into Japanese since Jun did not speak French.

'Witnesses on the platform thought she was praying . . . The train made it half way across the Pont du Passy, before it stopped.'

He gave the paper to me so I could read the front page for myself, as if by my reading the words, the tragedy became real. I noticed immediately that he kept the fine details to himself, like how the flanges of the train's wheels had cut through Yumiko's shoulders like a guillotine. Her arms had dropped down beside the track, detached.

Yuichiro took a slither of tartine from the plate in the middle of our table. The red jam gleamed with what light ricocheted off the limestone walls rising above us. The café, located down a lane off the Carrefour Alésia, had only four tables outside its window. While Yuichiro preferred the grander cafés of the boulevards, the Café Rotonda, the Café Flora, Jun preferred to eat in such out of the way places. He said he liked the cooler air.

Jun listened to the news, chewing his fecelle with slow rotations of his jaw. He ate in silence most days, his eyes half shut as if concentrating on some tune in his head. Yuichiro was a different man altogether. Whenever eating breakfast at the Houdini, he would always look up at the limestone walls, to the strip of blue sky above. The spire of the Church Saint-Pierre-de-Montrouge burned white with the glare of the morning sun just beyond the lane's entrance. The August heat would always creep down the walls, until the lane became stifling with a heat that lasted well into the night.

'I wonder if there will be an investigation?' Yuichiro said.

It is not a well-known fact that both Kozu brothers painted. What fewer know is that of the two brothers, Jun was the better technician. When he wasn't at the small hospital his father had set up for him in Hakodate, after he had left military service, Jun would spend hours bent over a desk, sharpening pencils with an old fruit knife and lining them up in order of use. Jun had been a surgeon for the Japanese Red

Cross during the campaign against the Russians, but the quiet of the small practice was better suited to his temperament, or so he said. Six years had passed since he cut and sowed the meat of soldiers, who cried under his knife, more with the shame of living, of not falling into the honourable silence of the battlefield, than with the pain. As a young man, he had wanted to study cartography at the Tokyo Technical School of Art, but had turned to medicine, after the school was forced to close by the traditionalist revival of the '90s. If it wasn't for the summons Yuichiro had sent him from Paris, Jun would have stayed put, listening to the wheezing lungs of the elderly and tending the broken bones of children.

What Yuichiro lacked in precision, he made up for in emotion, a trait that caused the Kozu family no end of embarrassment. Three years Jun's senior, Yuichiro had fled Hakodate to live and paint in Paris, filled with ambition – the dream – to become a great painter – the greatest Japanese painter in Europe. That he had fled his father's anger, after an incident with a fisherman's daughter, was not talked about in the Kozu family, though Jun later told me the story with relish. As it was, Yuichiro's responsibilities as eldest son meant little to him. Paris, city of art, philosophy, electric lights, was all that mattered.

But Yuichiro was well aware of his brother's prowess and so, the week before Jun arrived in Paris, Yuichiro unleashed a fresh rumour to infest the cafés and ateliers of Montparnasse. The word on the street was that a new Japanese face was to appear in the quarter. Not the face of a quiet mind with blank, nihilistic eyes, like so many of the other young Japanese artists in their dark suits, scribbling away in some *academie* or other, their fop teachers breeding into them an aesthetic the critics would then use to dismiss them as academicians. Such was their lot. It was no wonder I saw so many of them during the week, silent, brooding, pacing the corridors of the Louvre, instead of walking the streets outside. No. This new face would be crisscrossed with scars. A man, so the rumour went, who believed in the Anarchist maxim of 'propaganda of action' and wanted to extend its fingers over the throat of Art herself – Yuichiro had a penchant for hyperbole. Before Jun even stepped foot onto the limestone cobbles of the artists' quarter, Yuichiro had transformed the young doctor into a legend, a name debated in the cafés, at the edge of wine glasses.

Though I only met Yumiko in the flesh a couple of times, I got to know her form intimately. You see, during the month before Jun's arrival Yuichiro introduced me to his studies of the girl. It is true to say, I found her thinness repulsive.

Yuichiro had been seeing Yumiko behind her husband's back for about three weeks when I met him for breakfast at the Café Houdini. This was our Monday routine, as Mondays were the only day of a week the Louvre closed its doors to the public, freeing Yuichiro from his studies of the great masters, if only for a day. Yuichiro ordered coffee for the two of us. I drank the black liquid as best I could. I would have drowned the bitter taste with milk, just as Yuichiro did, but that would have upset my stomach. Though I had lived in Paris for almost a year by that time and had successfully trained myself to drink red wine, even to enjoy its taste, coffee always gave me a tremendous headache.

'I have brought you my sketches of Yumiko,' Yuichiro said and proceeded to lay down several sheets of cartridge paper on the table. 'What do you think?' I felt honoured to have the opportunity to offer my advice on a work in progress, but before I could offer my humble opinion, he continued, 'This girl, she will launch my name across Paris. "Kozu", they will call, my name echoing off the walls of the Salon, like the report of a gun!'

It seems strange to me now that I can sit here and talk to you of a time when any work by Kozu was less of interest for what would become his signature style, than his ability to ape the Japanese masters before him. You probably find such a time even more inconceivable than I, but, you can be assured, before the portrait your wife has shown such a keen interest towards was exhibited at the Salon Autumne, Yuichiro Kozu was little more than a copyist, albeit a copyist who managed to keep us living in fine apartments.

His arrival in Paris, five years before mine, could not have been more fortuitous. Japanese prints were still in vogue and many artists and intellectuals collected them by the hundred. With his ability to study and copy whatever he laid his eyes on, Yuichiro cashed in on this trend, this *Japonisme*, making a quick fortune by reproducing selected street scenes by Hokusai, famous landscapes by Hiroshige and the beautiful women of Utamaro. All of which he claimed were original. That was how I first made his acquaintance. With Yuichiro's deft eye for detail, a week or two of Parisian sunlight to fade the fresh inks and my contacts, we were set for success. He even made up some pieces from scratch, laying down just a few lines of ink and selling them off as rare sketches made by some great master on their deathbed.

But I digress.

I looked at those sketches Yuichiro had handed me,

finished my beverage and felt the first bangs of an approaching headache.

'Kozu-san,' I said to him, 'they are not quite what I would have expected.'

'What do you mean?' His hands closed into fists. 'Isn't she the most interesting subject you've seen in years? And she's Japanese to boot!'

'Is it not that she is uninteresting – she does have a most peculiar body, but . . .'

I spoke the truth. Yuichiro had skilfully rendered the body of a woman in thick swipes of charcoal, but this woman looked close to death. The very sight of her skeletal figure brought to mind those artists who in the late days of the Heian period would sketch the bodies of peasants dumped on the sides of roads.

I said to Yuichiro, 'She is so painfully thin, wherever did you find her?' and he told me about the Metro, of how he thought I would recognize her. 'She's Masahiro Saiki's wife,' he said.

Of course I knew of Saiki. At the time he was the only Japanese artist the French critics approved of. That was reason enough for the conservatives back here to reject him; and well, I don't mean to be scandalous, but Masahiro Saiki's lifestyle has become the stuff of legend. The tales of his Russian mistresses are proof of that. From the elegance of his nudes, though, one would never have assumed he was bold and short, with the thick shoulders of a judo champion and the face of a poor boxer.

Yuichiro explained to me how she hadn't eaten properly for months, saying that the food in Europe didn't agree with her. 'It's too rich,' she would say, and true enough, I saw her force down a lunch once, only to become violently ill afterwards.

I took another look at the sketches, holding each image up to the sky, one by one, so as to illuminate Yuichiro's slashed lines from behind. The light around the café was growing stronger by the minute and with it, my headache intensified. I tried to relax, to enjoy the burnt earth scent of their charcoal, but something nagged me about Yuichiro's composition. Before I knew it, I had sullied my jacket with blackened fingers.

I asked whether she had a lovely face, for it was unclear from the sketches.

'It's hard to tell,' Yuichiro replied. 'She has lovely hair. She wears it down – like those renegade girls one reads about in newspapers sent from home.'

I asked myself: where was the so-called cherry blossom he had boasted of? Maybe I should I have kept my objections to myself – I have spent much time since those days, wondering whether I should have kept true to my upbringing and not appraised Yuichiro's effort so directly. As it was, his talk of the girl's hair clarified my doubts.

Now, I beg your pardon, sir, but I take it that an esteemed and knowledgeable gentleman like your good self is familiar with the work of Kawanabe Kyosai? I am sure you'll agree that he was the last of the great Japanese print artists – for no other figure, with the decline of that delicate form, has risen to match the skills of such a man. This was especially so when it came to his pictures of *yurei*. Ghosts. My own nurse told me ghost stories when I was a child, so as to stop me leaving my futon on hot summer nights. Her favourite story was of a nameless *yurei* Kyosai had rendered, an image she had seen in my father's study. I can still hear her nasal way of speaking (so far removed from the soft grace of my mother's), as she warned me of that ghost of ghosts, of how it wandered the night, the hair of a severed head clenched between its teeth.

Though I digress, and excuse my impropriety, I am privileged to say that my father knew Kyosai in person. Knew him well. And once, while I helped him dry his brushes, the cicadas' call a low hum from the twilight outside, my father told me how Kyosai had confided in him a secret – the reason for why his ghoulish scenes chilled the public so. The great master told my father a story from his youth, of how he had found a severed head on a riverbank. With the detachment of undiscovered genius – that was how my father put it – the nine-year-old Kyosai took the grim curio home. Of course, his parents were outraged and made him cast it into the river. But before he did so, he had the wherewithal to draw that unique trophy from every angle.

That blue-sky morning, sat at the Café Houdini, I told Yuichiro the same anecdote. His reaction was curious. He looked puzzled at first, until I pointed out that Yumiko's emaciated shoulder blades, the way her spine cleaved her ribs in two, for all the sketches of Yumiko were from behind, reminded me of Kyosai's image.

I regretted my words instantly. Yuichiro ordered another cup of coffee, drank it in silence, brooding on my words. The pain behind my right eye increased with every wordless moment that passed between us. I should have kept my thoughts to myself.

Dishonesty aside – for Yuichiro was not one to bother himself with ethics – try to imagine how a man with such raw talent could manage in a world where it seemed every fresh breeze, rising off the Seine, bore within its vapour the germ of some great new idea, a new way of seeing. Fresh-faced youth gorged their appetites on Van Gogh, the brushwork of Cézanne, the personality of Picasso, while he knew himself a fraud. Compared to the rest of us, he was a rich man, yes, and a handsome man, but in his own eyes, Yuichiro Kozu was nothing more than a mimic, a glorified apprentice. And what was more, a Japanese apprentice at that.

I apologized and tried to extradite myself from my blundering. I said that, on second thought, I had been mistaken, that it was the dusting of charcoal across the paper that reminded me of Kyosai. The hazy effect it produced brought to mind that ghostly vestige of Kyosai's *yurei* because it reminded me of Asian light, murky and wet. It was not a Parisian light.

Yuichiro stared at me as I blathered, finally standing up when I started to repeat myself. 'You will meet her yourself,' he said.

I agreed, ashamed that I had caused him such vexation.

The next morning at eight, I arrived at Yuichiro's apartment on the corner of the rue de l'Alboni, where the Metro tracks glide out over the Seine. I expected him to show me through to the parlour, the spacious room, split in two by a set of finely wrought Japanese doors, the fretwork of which twisted and burst to the interlinking rhythms of cherry blossoms and their branches. Tatami-matting, too, covered the floor, so that in the summer heat, the room was filled with the green fragrance of home. That was where I joined him when we met with prospective clients, his lithe body hidden beneath a black kimono. He always looked smaller amongst those folds of black silk. As it was, he met me at the door, dressed in a grey pinstriped suit. He didn't stop and was halfway down the second flight of stairs before I caught him up.

I followed him outside and up the steps to the Passy Station. He instructed me to buy a first-class ticket and checked his watch. I eyed the mouth of the tunnel beyond the end of the platform. I used the line often to visit Yuichiro, but always got off at Passy. I never liked the idea of being shot into the tunnels beneath the Right Bank, like some virus injected into an artery.

A train pulled into the station and we boarded. As if entering the confines of a stage, Yuichiro stepped up to a woman sat next to the doors, her face covered by the brim of her hat. She looked to be sleeping. 'I am Yuichiro Kozu. I paint cats,' he said. The girl looked up. I remember that moment distinctly. The train passed into the tunnel and the lights flickered. Her face was at once Japanese and not. I don't know why, but her mouth, lips red and smiling in that instant of the lights' failure, brought to mind a poem by Basho: the one where the heron's shriek illuminates a flash of lightning.

Unaccustomed, as I was at the time, to speaking to women from my own culture, I bid the girl a good morning, hoping she would turn her face, those lips, towards me. She did not. Her energy, intense, as if connected to the currents that pulled the train through the underbelly of the French capital, was directed at Yuichiro. So this was Yumiko, I thought. Yuichiro sat down beside her, offering her a cigarette. I was left to stand. She lit the tobacco herself with practiced movements, took a drag and looked me up and down, a movement of the eyes I had never seen a Japanese woman do before, let alone do so with such vigour. 'Don't you work for the consulate?' she asked. I explained that I, like Yuichiro, was an artist. She scoffed.

Yuichiro interjected, 'My friend here is a famous man, you know, a working man. You've seen his pictures, Yumiko, of that I'm sure. You just don't know it.' Though his face was earnest, I knew Yuichiro was mocking me. You see, during my time in Europe, my only success came, not by exhibiting at the Salon, but from my commercial practices. My proficiency with a brush, as it was back then, along with a connection of my father's at the Japan Steamship Company, gained me a commission painting the images for that company's advertisements.

It is a shame that you have not been to Europe

yourself sir, but I am sure you must have seen one of the advertisements I painted. Yuichiro hated such posters. He saw them as emblems of the academic style our countrymen were enslaved to. That was how I originally met him, when he declared to me, as I sat reading in a chair in the Jardin du Luxembourg that I should paint whores and sheep, whores and sheep only, he told me.

'Do you think,' I still remember him asking me, 'do you think Japanese women look like sheep? I think you do, what with those elongated eyes you always give them. Not one of your portraits has any expression in spite of the smile you paint onto their lips.' The spring sunshine was bright on the white gravel, the surface of the Fontaine de Medicis, and I found myself unable to disagree.

What I am trying to say, sir, is that Yuichiro believed my portraits to be momentous failures. Standing on that train, watching Yumiko puff on her cigarette, as she studied her own reflection in the window, I could understand why.

After we had passed out of Boissiere, Yuichiro moved to a seat across from Yumiko. 'This is how I want to paint you,' he said, 'here on the Metro. I'll call it *Train and Chrysanthemums* or something similar. You'll have chrysanthemums on your kimono, gold ones like the crest of the Emperor – yes – gold over white silk!'

Still smarting from his mocker, I told him that I hadn't figured him for a genre painter, at which Yuichiro shook his head. He would construct the carriage around Yumiko, he exclaimed, with the shadows creeping out from the black walls of the tunnels beyond the windows, falling across her neck, collar bone, the top of her sternum; she would be wearing only the outer layer of her kimono, its white silk resembling a funeral gown. Yumiko would glow – an ethereal energy to match the invisible powers that hurled the train underground.

The train pulled into Etoile. All three of us alighted. I was still unsure of where we were headed, until I followed Yuichiro and Yumiko, walking arm in arm like some Parisian couple, onto a Line 1 train. From there, I assumed we were making our way to the Louvre.

'I do not want to wear a white kimono,' Yumiko said once aboard. 'I do not want to wear anything at all. I want you to paint me as a nude.'

Well, you can imagine the flush that coloured my cheeks at such an outburst. And on the Metro of all places! I could have sworn the other passengers, those Frenchman in their collars, and neckties, the lady who sat close by, a peacock's feather in her hat, could understand what Yumiko had said. Only, they were too shocked too look in our direction. I was reminded of that train journey a few years later, when those upstart New Women, you remember the ones, caused a scandal by visiting Yoshiwara, the pleasure district, and drinking French liquor in its bars!

Yumiko must have noticed my discomfort because she then said to me in French, 'Why uncle, was it not because of women's flesh that you became a painter?'

An old man along from us chuckled at this perversion of Renoir's sacred proclamation. I decided there and then to get off at the next station, to escape this demon in woman's clothing – I would not play Benvolio to her Mercutio.

To inflict further embarrassment upon me, she carried on with her offensive, turning to Yuichiro and saying, 'I already have an idea on how I want you to paint me: there will be a system behind my pose – something more than just a vase of arranged flowers and an umbrella.'

She thought for a moment, sucking smoke into her lungs, before she continued with her manifesto, catching glimpses of herself in the window behind a spellbound Yuichiro, seeming to enjoy the shapes her words took as smoke, 'Consider my lines, my profile: the triangle of my legs as I hold them before me, hands on my knees, arms an inverted triangle.' She raised her chin. 'My eyes look upwards, as if at some distant horizon. Your idea of using the Metro is good, inspired even – I want to gaze up towards a carriage window, I want the viewer to ask, 'Does she gaze at that space between her own reflection and the world beyond the window, one haunting the other?''

At that point, before she could continue, the train came to halt at Concorde. I fled.

You would never think, would you sir, that this girl, hanging so serenely before us, could be the same girl who said such ignominious things? I try to remember what she looked like that day, but all I can remember is her smile – her rouge lips. You see, although it is my business to collect faces, to pass them on, so to speak, I have great difficulty recalling them, if they are not close at hand. That was one of my many failings as a young artist. I could not paint from memory, nor abstract the qualities of the many faces I had seen into some personal vision of the ideal. That, I guess, was why my women looked like sheep. After Yuichiro's criticisms, I spent hours in the Louvre, copying firsthand the single works of Valequez, Rubens, Rembrandt, which hung in the Salon Carré, outnumbered by their Italian competitors. But once I left those hallowed halls, to catch one of those motorized buses that lined up outside the

Denon Gate, I could only recall the visages of murky ghosts.

I guess this is another reason for why – and I do not mean to be coy here – I am reticent to part with Kozu's portrait of Yumiko. To no longer have her face in the gallery, watching over me as I talk of other works, their artists and their models, rivalries and confederations, would be like seeing her far out at sea, drifting away. A particular feature of a face – a nose, chin, a smile – I can recall with ease. If you asked me to sketch out a likeness of the Mona Lisa, or more to the point Yuichiro Kozu himself, I would have to locate a magazine or a textbook from which to copy. That is, apart from his eyes. Those I could present you within minutes, as if I had plucked them from his head moments before you walked through my door and made a study of them. It took Kozu's portrait and, more specifically, Jun's arrival in August for me to realize how hard Yuichiro's eyes could be.

He wore glasses you see, Yuichiro, round-rimmed spectacles that, with his moustache, and height (made greater by the bowler hat he wore out) gave him a rather European look. An Occidental profile I think he enjoyed. He rarely took them off, blaming his poor eyesight on the nights spent as a youth sketching and painting, the only time he could practise without his father becoming suspicious. I know it is rude to speak so openly of a son neglecting his father, but you must understand: Paris was intoxicating. Its scent was in our noses, our hair, before the steamer docked at Le Havre or Marseille, even before boarding the train to Yokohama. It was borne in the skies of the Van Goghs or Matisses we gazed at in bookstores, their clouds smelling of turpentine.

It is strange how one remembers one thing and forgets another. Like those moments one knows, deep in the heart, will be a fulcrum in our lives. Proust knew it – would spend hours reflecting on an imperfect glance of a woman who flashed by his cab. I knew from Jun Kozu's opening remark to me the night I met him, he would change my life. 'I have my nose,' was what he said, looking up from a cup of tea as white as the tie of his evening dress.

But forgive me. I was talking about Yuichiro's eyes and now, here, Jun's nose. When really, at this point, I'm more interested in recalling the night in which Yuichiro introduced me to Jun, himself. Suffice, it was the night I first met Jun that illuminated me to how cold Yuichiro's stare could be. How penetrating. You'll understand why I've jumped ahead presently, when I tell you I met Dr. Junosuke Kozu on a Tuesday evening few Parisians will ever forget! For reasons lost to me now, I did not go to the Louvre that day. What I remember is the call of the newspaper vendors, announcing the release of the evening editions. The city was changed in an instant: The Mona Lisa, *La Jonconde* herself, was gone. Stolen.

I was amazed. Not three days before, I had walked past that girl, as I had done countless times before, collecting my easel from the warden who manned the store cupboard in the Salon Carré and joined the other copyists studying the paintings therein. Yuichiro would often join me there, if he was not preparing for a sale. He would never take up a brush though, choosing to sit there instead, staring at the pictures, making his own mental etchings.

Though I had never painted De Vinci's lady myself, I never dreamed that she would be lost. The sense of shock was palpable on the streets: each man that passed me seemed lost in his own newspaper. The cafés were abuzz with conjecture.

I hurried to the Houdini, to the gossip and theories of the regulars.

It was a beautiful evening, what I have since come to call a silver dusk. All those who have lived in Paris know such evenings, when the sun is low, cutting underneath the ceiling of summer storm clouds; light rebounds, down off the cumulus grey, down into the city, off its limestone and up again. The effect is magical. Every surface beyond the orange lamps of the café awning, is touched by mercury. The air has a thickness, like coal smoke, like that which drifts up from the tugboats on the Seine, the little ones whose funnels collapse down at the bridges. One would hope for rain at such moments. Not because the evening air was unpleasant, but because a thunderous downpour would leave the streets, the cobles, the trees, the fruit carved into the facades of buildings, shining. Such a café night, with the heavens fleshly opened and purple above, is the essence of Van Gogh's *Café under Gaslight*. A night without any black.

Such was the night of the theft and my first encounter with Jun. (I told you I would get here). The wine was warm on my lips, when I noticed Yuichiro with a shorter man outside the café's window. Both were dressed in formal evening wear. From the stranger's rigid gait and black hair, I instantly knew him to be Japanese. I had no idea I was looking at the so-called anarchist painter of Montparnasse. I took my glass and walked out into the warm air to join them.

'We were just discussing my painting of Madame Saiki,' Yuichiro said by way of a greeting. I liked the way he did that in front of other Japanese men, foregoing formalities and talking to me like an artist of significance. Fournier, the Houdini's ancient waiter, brought me a chair and I joined the table. It was as I sat down that I looked directly at the stranger's face, a visage brutally scarred. Jun must have noticed a change in my demeanour, for I had only just sat down when he introduced himself so memorably, following up with, 'I am fortunate . . . more so than others,' and an explanation, punctuated by sips of tea, of how he had arrived in Paris the day before, after spending an entire week in Marseille. The voyage had not agreed with him.

Jun's face was not an 'etching hatched of white lines,' as Yuichiro had put it, but a single shard of shrapnel had sculpted his flesh in the most fascinating way. Yuichiro told the story. Jun sat in silence. Apparently, the Russians had gunned for the aid station where Jun laboured under Mt. Taipo-shan, wounding him while he tended the wounds of others. It was a wide incision, cutting from beside the bridge of his nose down into his mouth, parting his top lip. I do not mean to be grotesque, to linger on a mark of valour, but whenever I try to picture Jun, I see his mouth, curtain-lipped. His teeth. Little else. He never smiled in my presence and yet, there they were, his golden incisors, on display for all to see.

Yuichiro went on to tell me about how, earlier that evening, Jun and he had gone to watch a live demonstration of a machine that could pierce the flesh without the need of a wound. The image it presented to the stunned audience was the perfect copy of the bones that lay underneath.

Something about Yuichiro's words brought Jun back to life. 'Have you seen the portrait he speaks incessantly of?' he asked of me, his Japanese vernacular. I didn't know whether he felt the normal formalities unneeded in that foreign land, or that my station as an artist, in the midst of building a career, was beneath him.

Believing he was talking of the stolen De Vinci, I told Jun I had seen the Mona Lisa on many occasions.

He cut me off with, 'No, no, not that painting. I am talking about this portrait of a Japanese girl. It seems to have possessed him, he talks of it so often!'

I looked at the rim of my glass, said that I had not, though Yuichiro had shown me some of his charcoal studies for it. My exact words are lost to me, but I explained how I thought Yuichiro's choice of setting, the busy Metro carriage, was inspired. To gaze upon a naked Japanese beauty amongst the bustle of commuters, was the manifestation of the city's cosmopolitan allure. Yumiko would become a symbol of the body universal – that gift of the flesh erstwhile hidden beneath our decorations, the picturesque accessories of custom. I tried to make my voice as animated as possible, intense, without appearing vulgar.

Jun nodded, 'You should see it I think. Maybe some-one else can tell my brother what a fool he is.'

I begged Jun's pardon, while Yuichiro ordered three brandies.

'His picture,' Jun continued, 'this so-called masterpiece. I'll admit the carriage is technically proficient, but the girl, that supposed Japanese girl? She is a monstrosity.'

'Always the academician,' Yuichiro said, turning his eyes, those cold, cold eyes, upon me. He had removed his glasses and sat there, leaning back, hands folded behind his head. The brandies arrived and Jun's tea was tidied away.

Yuichiro said, 'As I said before, you must consider the picture's balance. It is wonderful, with her back arched over her legs, her ribs cutting across the centre frame as vertical lines. Must I explain this every time? All lines rise upward; her tones are light, the colour of her skin pink, warm. She is not deathly white, as our tradition would have her. She is maybe ill, but she knows she is alive; skin and bones, yes, but consumed by life, her own thoughts, her reflection hanging over the city passing by outside. I've not given her an out-line either: nothing holds her together, down; her halo merges with the carriage!'

'Pretty words,' Jun said. 'But words are the work of a Sunday painter. Not an artist.'

Yuichiro blew a cloud of smoke into the silver light of the lane. I watched it change colour as it rolled into the shadows and nothingness. 'Of course you would say that, when, it is the idea brother – and not its execution – that matters.'

I was stunned, thrilled. Never had I heard my own countrymen so animated, and in a public place, too. I couldn't help myself and blurted out, 'What is it about Saiki's wife that so offends your sensibilities, Kozu-sensei?'

'Her face. Her body I do not care for,' Jun began. 'But her face . . . it is a blasphemy. We sit here in a city mourning the loss of one girl's smile and my brother thinks he can replace it with one of his own.'

As though part of a play, at that moment a feminine voice addressed our table in French, 'My friend and I were wondering whether we could join you.'

It was Yumiko! And she was not alone. On her arm was a man with a scraggy beard that matched the colour of his tweed suit. I knew him to look at – he was an Italian artist, a sculptor, rumoured to store his shit under his bed. He reeked of garlic sausage.

Yumiko said something about the great theft and how Montparnasse was the place to be on such a night.

Without asking permission, the Italian sat down

beside me and addressed Jun, 'You there, Jap, I know you.' He was drunk.

Yuichiro smiled, refusing, or so it looked, to acknowledge Yumiko. 'Monsieur, who could you possibly know here?'

'Him,' said the beast, pointing at Jun. 'You're that phantom Jap painter.'

Jun looked around the table, but it was left to me to translate the Italian's accusation. Wiping his hands with a napkin, Jun went to take his leave, but Yuichiro stopped him, saying, 'Let's see what this fellow has to say about my idea. What impeccable timing Yumiko.'

Jun took a second look at the girl. 'This is Yumiko?' he asked, 'I wouldn't have recognized her. Not having seen that monstrosity, at least.'

Yumiko bowed, her movements greased with insolence, '*Sensei.*'

The Italian called over to Fournier, demanding he bring a fresh bottle of wine. He would drink with us tonight. Yuichiro went to introduce himself, but was cut off. The Italian knew who the print-seller from the rue du l'Alboni was. He had no interest in Japanese prints, nor any other wares that Yuichiro wished to proffer. What interested him was Jun, what such a man with a face so scarred had to say about the nature of painting beautiful faces.

Jun did not respond immediately. I can still picture him there, nursing his glass, studying Yumiko, the fading daylight flashing over his gold teeth.

The wine arrived. It rained.

'Well, sir,' Jun said at last, 'I believe that abstraction is tantamount to laziness. It is nothing new, the artwork of our nation is emptied of detail, is full of lies. Your great Leonardo knew that.'

I translated.

The Italian smiled and shook his mane, slapping Jun on the shoulder with a dirty hand. Jun studied the mark it left on the white silk of his scarf.

'That is not very revolutionary! Yumiko has told me all about you, Phantom. She told me many things, indeed. She said you would be here tonight,' he pointed to a small table beside the piano, the Houdini's only piece of substantial future other than its counter, 'we've been watching!'

'And what has she told you?' Yuichiro asked, enjoying the blooms he had obviously planted.

The Italian filled his glass, preparing for a story as if it were his own. Wine pooled in his beard. Over his shoulder he called out whether any person could tell him how to calculate the proportions of a figure study. A voice called back from the night and rain beyond the awning, 'Seven times – the body should be seven times the length of the head!'

The Italian stared hard at Jun, 'Nearly. Isn't that true my friend?' His voice fell to a whisper, 'A body, from crown to sole, is seven and a half times the length of the head. Vitruvius taught us that, didn't he? Yumiko tells me that you put old Vitruvius to the test, Jap; that at you measured some decapitated Russian with his own head! Is that true?'

Jun leaned forward. 'It was at the Battle of Taishan,' he said, his tone even. 'Vitruvius was quite astute in his calculations.'

Well, sir, I didn't know what to do. I reshaped Jun's words into French. I had heard Yuichiro boast of his brother's unconventional methods before, but I never expected them to be true.

Jun then asked Yumiko how such a declaration made her feel. He couldn't imagine he had caused her any offense, what with her husband's notorious love of Russian dancers. Saiki's works were full of them, he was told. Was it true that the famed Masahiro Saiki had never asked his own wife to model for him?

I watched Yumiko's lips curl into a smile, which she made no attempt to cover with her hand. The expression in her eyes is impossible to describe – it was not quite angry, not quite blank, either.

Before she could retort, Jun exclaimed, 'There it is!

In this light it is so plain to see! That is what you failed to capture in your picture brother: that is the face of a Japanese woman. You have spent far too long in the Louvre; far too long seeing the world through white eyes. Look at her face. How can you not see it? I could demonstrate what I meant if I had a skull specimen with me!'

And so it was spoken. At some point, we moved inside the café. The Italian, filthily drunk, told us stories about his childhood in Livorno. Looking around, to see that the place was empty, he lowered his voice and asked, 'Do you know why this place is called the Houdini?'

I made a quip about how my money always vanished after drinking there, to which Yumiko belched out a laugh, the likes of which I have never heard emitted from a lady since. Yuichiro lifted his head and patted me on the back, as if he had been awake all along. Jun did not laugh.

The Italian called over to Fournier. The old waiter obviously had a soft spot for the wild-headed sculptor because, after wiping his hands on his apron, he came over to us and uncorked a bottle of brandy. Before he could pour himself a drink, I took the bottle and performed the action for him, as is our custom.

'Tell them about the Houdini's magical powers,' the Italian asked the waiter.

Now, sir, many nowadays think the café was named after that great illusionist, as a witty way to commemorate the manner in which he died, struck in the stomach as he was while being sketched by an art student the other year. Fournier made a great show of coming round front and locking the doors before he explained that the Houdini was called the Houdini because it shared the key ingredient of any great conjurer's trick: it had a trap door. Or rather, an access shaft made and abandoned by the Inspectorate of the Mines. A person could enter in the small café, and disappear, maybe to reappear somewhere else.

'And why should trap doors interest us?' Jun asked me to enquire.

The Italian replied in Fournier's stead, 'The Empire of Death, my friend! There are catacombs beneath our feet, places where you can play with as many skulls as you like. I know: I've been there. And you've put me in the mood for adventure.'

He winked at Yumiko.

I have thought about the events that followed that call to the catacombs many times, to the extent that I am no longer sure of the accuracy of my memory, like a Chinese apprentice copying the work of his master. What I remember is Fournier leading us down into the kitchen, a windowless room, its darkness absolute, where he handed each of us a candle. Like a line of the pious, we received our flames in turn. There were some low tunnels after that (in which Yuichiro had to bend at his waist), two stone stair cases and cobwebs – thick miasmas that tugged at one's hair like the sticky fingers of children. The subterranean coolness was a relief after the heat above.

When we came to a wider tunnel, Fournier announced that we had reached the catacombs, pointing to a rough black line that ran along the ceiling. If we were to become separated, he explained, we were to follow that lifeline to an exit. The Italian pushed through to the front of our expeditionary force, his candle's flame reflecting off Jun's teeth.

The absence of light makes it difficult to recount our passage. Candlelight on chiselled limestone; the closeness of our breath; feet scraping wet gravel: all evoked a sensation within one's heart, not a picture to the eye. Every now and then, the echoes of our passage would widen around us, bounding off into the black, into tunnel mouths left to their mystery.

We came upon two black-painted columns, sometime later, a white obelisk design painted on each. The inscription on the transom they held aloft read: 'Halt! This here is the empire of death.'

Genius confronted us on the other side of the doorway, a sight I cannot give shape to with my descriptions – I wonder if even Akutagawa could? Bones, tens of thousands of them, were stacked in piles jutting out from the cavern walls. Layer upon layer upon layer: their numbers meaningless. The macabre architecture was a marvel, its craftsmanship impressing itself upon one's reason. But the art of it struck a deeper cord. Edging along the bone banks, candle at arm's length, my face level with the crania crested dams, the hollows within them filling with light, I admired the strange, brutal patterns which came into view: a wheel of long bones, spokes crowned with skulls; a heart of skulls; an altar's cross.

Beside me, the Italian took up a skull and, despite its missing teeth and jawbone, pretended to bite Yumiko's shoulder with it. Yumiko giggled with delight. 'It's so light,' she said, taking the white orb from his hands. Yuichiro made a quip in Japanese about its similarities with the pronounced forehead of an Italian. The sculptor kissed Yumiko's hand as in response to those words he could not have understood, and took her into the next chamber. Yuichiro followed.

I returned to Jun, who was muttering to himself

about how the meat and liquid gave a head its weight, his body a silhouette, hunched over the lip of stack. With his candle so close to the wall, his hands were lost in the mire of shadows. I enquired as politely as I could what it was he was doing, looking as he did into my eyes like some soothsayer, a sham Hamlet.

'Looking for a mandible,' he replied. 'To make a complete human vertex. There are things I must prove to my brother.'

After hearing the story of how the doctor had used a Russian head as a measure, I decided to help Jun fulfil his bizarre quest, digging my hands into the mound of bones. I can still remember the sensation, the lightness, which brought to mind the shells of cicadas. I discarded sheath after sheath, each with the surface texture of rain-pitted limestone, in my search for the more substantial grit of teeth.

Yuichiro rejoined us. At that moment I noticed the absence of Yumiko and the sculptor's giggling, which until then had reached us from the adjoining chamber through waves of echoes. Engaged as he was with his search, I thought Jun had no interest in Yumiko's behaviour and was content for her to do as she pleased with the *gaijin*. Or so I thought, until, quite abruptly, he stood up straight, receding as it seemed into the darkness.

'Do not trouble yourself,' he whispered. 'Do you think a fish knows that it is wet? It may know the sensation of the air when it jumps to catch a fly, but, in a flash, it is back underwater, dreaming about the world above.'

Yuichiro's breathing slowed and he threw down a tibia with a chuckle. 'You know,' he said, 'at last you say something that makes sense.'

At some point, Yuichiro said that we should give up the hunt for Jun's trophy of a mandible and leave, adding, 'Do you think Saiki will miss his beloved wife, if we leave her down here with all the other skeletons? You never know, she might feel at home down here.'

I do not wish to dwell upon what Yumiko and the Italian got up to in that other chamber, stared at by the hollow eyes of the dead, but when they returned Jun addressed the sculptor, saying that we should return to the surface. 'This has been quite the experience, sir,' he said.

My translation complete, the wild-haired man bowed, his exaggerated movements extinguishing the flame of his candle. Yumiko lit his flame with her own, drawing her face close to his as she did so.

Of the journey back to the Houdini's cellar I remember nothing other than the spectre of Fournier's sleeping form when we re-entered the kitchen. It was such a shock to see him there, his body whole and thin, his white hair glowing in the muted light of our candles, that Yumiko gave out a startled cry. The old man did not stir.

Yumiko asked whether she should wake him.

'The Houdini was not called the Houdini for nothing,' the Italian said, mimicking the waiter's southern accent. 'In an hour he will have to open the café – let him lay there.'

The rain had passed and the morning light reflected off the puddles in the lane, their edges cutting blue slithers between the cobbles. The lane smelt cold. Yumiko said something about a bath and the Italian, who seemed shorter when sober, grunted. His lips, black with dried wine, gave him the look of a tubercular apostle, his message and lungs spent. The two of them no-longer linked arms.

I went to take my leave, but Jun stopped me, saying that we should all pay a visit Yuichiro's apartment.

'I trust that Yumiko is still to view her own portrait?' he asked.

Yuichiro shook his head. No, she had not yet seen the painting. Yumiko clapped her hands and implored the sculptor to come with us to the Right Bank. We should take the train. The Italian made some excuse about an appointment later that afternoon. He needed sleep to prepare for it. Yumiko's expression turned crestfallen, but her smile never faded.

Without another word to her lover, she took Yuichiro by the arm and led him out onto the avenue. At the entrance to Alesiá, that station I am told was named after a great battle between the Gauls and the Romans, the Italian crossed the road and headed northeast. I never spoke to him again, though I saw him from a distance a couple of times and I know he saw me. Two of his works, sir, now hang in this gallery. Ask me to show them to you sometime.

It wasn't until we waited at the platform edge that I felt conspicuous, accompanied as I was with such a strange band of Japanese. Petty businessmen and clerks were on their way to work and there I was beside two Orientals in dishevelled evening dress, cuffs red with wine like surgeons, Yuichiro impassive, Jun brooding; and Yumiko, a painfully thin exotic without a hat (at some point she must lost it!), her black hair gleaming over her breasts, eyes glazed as if in a daydream. I felt every face on the platform turn towards us, whether with scorn or curiosity, I cannot say, shame bringing me close to tears. We did not speak.

At last we passed over the green waters of the Seine, shimmering like a vision by Matisse, the Eiffel Tower tall and emitting its invisible radio waves out over the world. We alighted at the Passy Station and I stumbled down its steps as if still drunk. Though no longer under the spotlight as it were, I felt something was chasing us; that at any moment a hoard of Parisians would surround us and throw us in the great green ribbon below Yuichiro's building, leaving our bodies to wash up, rank and rotten, on some sandbank at Le Havre.

Sat beneath the fretwork doors of Yuichiro's parlour, a glass of *sake* held between my trembling fingers, the tension finally evaporated. I lay down, looking up at those wooden blossoms. How perfect they were; Yuichiro must have had them handcrafted back at home and shipped halfway around the world. Jun sat crossed-legged beside me, while Yumiko stood at the bay window, looking out.

It took Yuichiro a short while to transport his canvas from studio to parlour; he didn't want any help. Yumiko's image was concealed beneath a cotton bed sheet, and I expected Yuichiro to make a great ceremony over the impromptu unveiling. As it was, he leaned the canvas against the fireplace and pulled off the sheet.

How to explain what happened next? Yumiko shook off the reverie which had pulled her eyes to the city outside, and dropped to her knees, speechless.

The picture was as Yuichiro had explained the night before. Yumiko, clutching her knees, looked outward towards a Metro carriage window. She was nude. The shadows from the tunnel did not spread across her naked form, though: what confronted one was an ultramarine sky, vast despite the window, breaking over purple-slated roofs, the limestone beneath them burnt-orange. The balance was striking: lines, straight and formidable, from the backs of the seats, to the highlights of Yumiko's ribs – all were angled towards that sky, infinite in their bearing, as Seurat had once theorized. Yumiko was beautiful, in a Gauguin kind of way, at once warmed and drained by that gaze towards blazing colour, her own body bright like those of the facades.

I applauded the masterpiece and its master, the painting was more achieved than I could have imagined from Yuichiro's sketches. I looked to Jun, to watch his reaction to the portrait, for I could not fathom why he had taken such offence at Yuichiro's vision the night before at the Houdini. Was it not the case in our modern world that, if the artist felt it to be so, he could paint the sun green? Would such a vision have to be wrong? Hadn't the catacombs below the greatest of European cities only confirmed the idea that we are bone beneath, our flesh destine to rot? If that was our destiny, shouldn't we look up at a green sun, or a thin girl of burnt-amber, for that matter, a girl looking to an ultramarine sky? Weren't we supposed to feel alive? Couldn't one of my own countrymen believe in that girl enough to allow us to believe in her too? To believe in ourselves?

Jun paced over to the window, unfolding his newspaper as he did so. He held up the front page beside Yumiko's face. De Vinci's smiling daughter of Florence looked back at us.

'You're continued blindness disappoints me, brother,' he said. 'Look at the angle of her jaw,' Jun demanded of Yuichiro, 'the curve of her ocular canals, their depth as they sweep along her cheek; look at the length of her teeth, how they extend the profile of her maxilla; the shallowness of her zygnomatic; the slope of her frontal bone – must I go on?'

'Please do,' Yuichiro said, lighting a cigarette, his only defence it seemed, when Jun went on the assault.

'Now, look back at this painting. What do you see?'

Yuichiro shrugged his shoulders; the question was redirected at me.

'A painting of a woman?' I answered, at a loss for what else to say.

'A painting of a white woman!' Jun threw back at us all. 'Yes, the hair may be black, her eyes a little narrow, but look at the face, its shape, its angles. They are not Japanese. All you have painted is a white woman, made-up for a fancy-dress ball. All this visionary rubbish is in vain if you cannot even see that your so-called art is not your own at all. If you cannot possess even the surface of an object, how can you attempt to evoke its spirit?'

Sir, how can I explain the power of Jun's words? It was as though a cloud had passed over the sun: the image of Yumiko, its brushstrokes and paint, remained physically unaltered, but its life force was stripped away. The Japanese girl was no longer of the Orient, but a parody in bright hues.

I looked at Yumiko's portrait and then at Yumiko: how different they were, it was true. How could I not have seen it before! Had I become so accustomed to copying the masters of that other culture myself, that I had allowed the colours, the pose, the system of Yuichiro's portrait to fool me. In that moment the fear that had chased me from the subway that morning, the fear that I thought dispelled by the smell of *tatami*, the taste of *sake*, the look of carved cherry blossoms, returned in force. I felt the weight of the city around me. The girl of the carriage, of the ultramarine sky and rooftops, was no Japanese beauty: she was constructed, thoroughly, through European grace. As such, she was a monster, a woman possessed. Yuichiro had captured the Western in Yumiko, without capturing Yumiko at all. The portrait repulsed me, just as Yumiko's manners had done so the day we first met on the Metro.

Moreover, the painting had fooled the artist himself and now, Yuichiro's failure confronted him, both in the image leaning against the mantelpiece and the girl who stood by the window. I can only imagine what went through his head at that moment, the doubts that set his dreams of being the best Japanese artist in Paris alight: if he displayed the picture in public, the critics, surely, would call his vision hackneyed, that the man from overseas lacked any originality of his own. That he was a copycat.

Yuichiro threw his glasses to the floor, moving toward Jun as if to strike, but before a blow could fall, Yuichiro stopped himself. He stared at the canvas and sunk to his knees in defeat.

'So I am an academician after all,' he said.

Jun, calm now, as if delivering a lecture, said, 'Brother, look at this girl – look at her. She is a lost soul. If you want to rescue her: give her back to herself. Show her –and those beyond these walls who incite an artist to do such violence upon her – that beauty isn't in disfigurement. Paint her! Is she not Japanese?'

Yumiko, who until this moment had remained silent, awestruck, much like myself at Jun's revelation of the European face that looked out from the portrait stood and gave out a wild laugh, like a soul possessed. With uncontrolled passion, she spat at Jun, 'I think Yuichiro has succeeded masterfully. He has looked into my heart and given shape, harmony, to my most inner desires. Yuichiro has painted me as I see myself. It is you who are blind.'

'Then you truly are lost. No wonder your husband favours his Russian whores. He might as well have married a foreigner.'

At such a levelling, Yumiko stormed out.

But Jun was not done. He left Yuichiro and me to stand in the parlour, while he followed the girl through the front door, onto the hallway landing, from where we could hear him shout down the stairwell, 'Yumiko-chan! Oi, Yumiko-chan! You may forget our country when fucked by a *gaijin*, but that won't make you white!'

He came back into the room and repositioned himself on the ledge of the parlour's open window. From his new vantage point, he must have caught sight of Yumiko as she fled up the stairs to the Passy Station, because again his voice boomed out, 'Enjoy your lie, Yumiko-chan! One silly artist may paint you white, but you'll never look anything other than Asian to this nation with cataracts!'

As far as I know, Yumiko kept her distance from Yuichiro after that episode. Never again did I see her at the Houdini, the Louvre, though I kept an eye out for her down every street I passed along, every park I sat in.

For a while, I thought she had perhaps joined her husband, who I knew to be touring the south coast. Then came that Monday when the Kozu brothers and I met for breakfast at the Houdini and Yuichiro handed me the paper, as I've already told you. I read first for myself that she was dead, self-murdered, her body wrapped in a white funeral kimono.

Yuichiro excused himself and returned to his apartment, I think now, to gaze upon his fatal portrait of Yumiko; his vision of what Yumiko had wanted to be, had willed him to paint, that image of what she never was.

The telegram arrived that same afternoon. Could I join him and Jun at the municipal morgue at 4.00 pm? A third party, to claim Yumiko's body, was needed. For reasons that I can only speculate about, it appeared Saiki had refused to claim her body.

Though I had known the morgue was open to the

public, I had never ventured inside it. What confronted me when I arrived left me more shocked than the crypts beneath Montparnasse. The grand high-ceilings, were filled with a strange scent like rotting apricots and behind glass doors, the bodies were laid out on rude beds. Somehow the overall effect was like that of a waiting room. I half-expected to run into the Great King Emma, the judge of the dead, at the end of the foyer. One or two of the visages behind the glass were calm and somnolent; others were frozen in a scream. Then there were those putrefied masses, stewed by the waters in which they had been found. To think Yumiko had wound up in such a place disgusted me.

To locate the Kozu brothers I had to solicit the help of a clerk. Jun greeted me cordially, like an old friend, and asked whether I had followed the instructions as they had been laid down in the telegram. I told them I had.

Yuichiro paced the room, a handkerchief pressed to his mouth and nose.

It was then I saw what remained of the painfully thin girl who had once described so vividly how she wished to be painted. Severed into pieces, she looked like a puzzle, like one of those dolls one used to see on sale for the instruction of children in expensive Ginza department stores; only she of course was not made of wood. Jun picked up her head alone and smeared it with chloride of lime, saying it was to prevent putrification. Her long hair was shorn; a pair of scissors lay on the tabletop where Jun worked.

I remember thinking how low I had sunk; how, in so short a time, I had ventured down a path leading me from one level of hell to another. I stood there, motionless, in that place where death seeped into the lungs, corrupting the soul from within, holding the leather travel bag, until he took it from me. Opening it, he proceeded to take one of the morgue assistants' aprons, a heavy black thing made of Indian rubber, and used it to line the bag's interior. Into that hole went Yumiko's severed head. He silenced the clerk's protests by asking me to explain how such practices are quite the norm in our country. We were to perform a burial right to set her soul at peace. I translated the lie, but the man did not look convinced. He exited the room, vowing to report us to his superiors. We made our escape. I cannot imagine the clerk's reaction on finding us fled, but he must have given up the chase, for nothing ever came of our leaving in such a manner.

As I replied to a similar question asked me by Akutagawa, I do not know why I accepted Jun's offer to catch a cab with them back to the rue de l'Alboni that afternoon. I do not expect you to understand why I couldn't abandon them. I mean, does one break ranks at the first volley? The first sight of blood? Yuichiro was wounded more than I. He had loved Yumiko in his way. If it were not for Jun, our steadfast commander, we both would have wavered from our route, casting that bag into the Seine.

When we stepped into the parlour, I could see that Jun had been busy that day. A line of scalpel blades and forceps, procured from who knows where, lay in a line on the edge of a square of black silk, which I recognized to be one of Yuichiro's kimono, folded neatly. The choice of material was an ingenious idea. Though Yumiko's lifeblood had long since drained away, Jun obviously didn't want waste from his specimen to distract his brother. Strange to think, isn't it sir, that a simple choice of work surface would be the source of Yuichiro's dark backgrounds for his portraits ever after.

Yuichiro left the room, only to return moments later, drying his face with a towel, his hair still wet. Under his arm he carried a sketchpad, a tin of pencils, too. He knelt down at the edge of the black square in *seiza*. Jun and I joined him. What a strange sight we were to behold, looking as we did, like guests at a tea ceremony.

Jun opened the travel bag.

The stench of rotting apricots and chloride of lime that ensued caused me to retch. Jun, the doctor, duly scolded me. Yuichiro, who sat there in silence, a blank expression on his face, rotated a pencil between his lips.

Whilst gently lifting the head from the bag to the silk, Jun instructed me in how I was to assist him, asking me to hand him a particular blade and certain forceps when the time called for them.

I think his words to Yuichiro were, 'Watch carefully. Sketch every detail. All those nuances the whites never see. Do not flinch.' For him, the girl had proven to be the strongest of us all; as such, we should honour her in this, our own way, a manner that would help her spirit find its bearing home. I listened to Jun's words and something struck me about the way he spoke, gesturing towards the head as he did so. He did not use Yumiko's name; in fact I had not heard either brother address Yumiko by her name since the morning I had seen her alive at the Houdini. The impression this imposed upon me was that, with her life force spent, Jun viewed Yumiko's severed head as an artwork, a piece of sculpture in itself, to be broken down and resembled on Yuichiro's pad.

The glare of the room's electric bulbs gave me a

headache, but I took in the remainder of Jun's orders and explanations with the morbid interest that lures one to a funeral – not that of a close relation, of course, but of a distant colleague, a man one did not know well.

I see my words offend you, sir!

In that case, I shall keep my story brief! Well, at last, Jun said, 'Shall we begin?' His tone was thoroughly professional, intrigued even. With such a calmness, I can still imagine how comforting he must have been on the battlefield, the shells falling all around, the wounded in awe of his discipline.

There is not much to tell after that: I handed Jun the tools he asked for and took them from his hand when he was done. Bile burnt the back of my throat, when Jun revealed the yellow layer of fat beneath the epidermis, but that was the only time. I steadied myself, holding firm, concentrating on the scratching sound Yuichiro's pencil made. The hum of the light bulbs eased my nerves.

Yuichiro's sketches were a marvel to behold – I still have two, from that very day, locked safely away. Their lines are so faint. As if Yuichiro were afraid to press any harder, to mark with fervour the morphological differences, as Jun called them, hidden away under muscle and capillary.

Ah, as for what happened to that first painting of Yumiko, the original? I do not know. As is well documented these days, it is this painting before you, his first truly Japanese work of art, which marks the great advancement of our country's painters into the 20th century. I do not need to tell you how Yuichiro began what was to become the great Japanese renaissance, a reclaiming of the truth from the Parisians who tried to bleed out our bloodline with their Western configurations of our Oriental beauties. My old friend would go on to paint over a hundred *bijinga*, and in doing so, he would take his place on that long path trodden by so many of our countrymen, deepening its ruts through his use of oils (no more pigment, no more ink); widening its girth with his rendering of facial nuances, those turns of bone and flesh that mark our race's place amongst the peoples of the world.

If you were to ask me where that earlier portrait was, that nude of Yumiko in which he saw her as she'd always wanted to see herself, I would ask your forgiveness, and say I don't know. But, and I do not mean to speak out of turn, if you push me I will confide in you something I have thought for many years: that the original of the rebellious girl I met that summer in Paris still exists, not stored away somewhere, but painted over, just as Picasso did with so many of his earlier works. Just think, sir, the ghost of that wild girl could be haunting the very flesh that caresses the cat your wife finds so charming!

That was the story I told to Akutagawa. I always hoped he would write about it someday, given how much he detested Kozu's portraits. But such speculation is by-the-by: I see your wife has come to collect you. I leave it up to you to decide whether or not to buy. The painting your wife so admires is one I have looked upon for, perhaps, too many years.

PART II

BOY WITH NO BIG TOE

The village of Nihongi, Nagano, 1947

In the moment before he laughed, the American bore an uncanny resemblance to the executioner from Toulouse-Lautrec's lithograph, *Au Pied de L'Échafaud*. 'Ah come on, Takayanagi,' he said. 'This little doozy's kept me warm all the way out from Suzuka.'

His joke went like this:

'A Japanese lieutenant-colonel walks into a French restaurant, the fancy kind with a maître'd. *Garcon! Garcon! Are you taking orders?* the Jap calls outs. And the maître'd replies: *Oui monsieur, I am taking orders, but not as well as you.'*

What could I say? As soon as I had caught sight of their jeep, its fresh layer of gloss the wrong shade of olive for our valley of burning leaves, I turned fleshless: a hungry ghost. I rubbed black mountain soil from my hands and the American coughed up another laugh, looking to his superior for support, a captain, whose uniform was so neat he could have been wearing an origami gown. The charcoal in our brazier popped but gave off little heat. The damp of the house seeped into me. How shabby the walls looked. How clean that uniform. My life was laid out in all its rudeness: the rotten *tatami*, the floorboards visible underneath, the fallen thatch wrinkling every surface.

The captain, tall and bored, was a Botticelli, from the master's *A Magis Adoratur*. Do you know the painting? Have you seen him standing there, Botticelli himself, on the edge of the Medici family, those brutal patrons of Florence? I could see the captain was a man who liked to listen – listen and remember all the words he's heard. A quiet man. His eyes a confrontation.

An apology slipped from my lips.

The captain waved his clipboard. There was a smile at some point. Enjoyment in the chase. He said, 'The Old Man wants to clean up any remnants of the old wartime cliques. We've been tasked with confiscating any documentary campaign pieces that may have been removed from Tokyo after the surrender. They're subversive. We are, after all, at peace.'

I called out to my wife for refreshments.

The captain refused to be distracted. 'We were hoping to locate some works by a war artist connected to your grandfather's gallery, a Yuichiro Kozu.'

I shrugged my shoulders, a gesture I thought my body had forgotten. 'Kozu was friends with Soutine, when my grandfather represented the Lithuanian in

Paris. That's how I met him, once or twice, after he became famous. He died during the war, I read; Soutine that is. Not enough medicine. That is all I know about Kozu.'

The American looked at me as though I wore a Noh mask. His subordinate grew impatient, demanding I hand over any Kozus in my possession, anything I may have removed from Army Headquarters in Tokyo before the surrender, anything stored at my grandfather's gallery. The house could easily be searched. My wife wouldn't like that at all, he said.

I bowed. 'The only artworks I own these days, gentlemen, I hang inside my head. As you can see, my wife and I are not very prosperous. Not anymore.'

'Ah yes: the fire.'

'The fire.'

At some point, my wife entered from the back and the captain instructed his man to mind his manners. Before each of us she delivered a steaming bowl of millet gruel, thickened with ground mountain yam, the vegetables I had just dug from the mountainside when the Americans' jeep rumbled into our valley. I offered our guests a *goza* mat to sit on, a reedy husk our neighbours had once used to dry their vegetables on. We ate in silence.

But neither the soup nor the silence appeased them

and soon the captain laid his chopsticks across the top of his bowl and said, mixing up my name, 'Now then, Mr. Takayanagi-san, why don't we have a little look in the woodshed?' They spent the better part of an hour overturning everything in the small space while my wife and I looked on. The war is over, but suspicions continue. So, Doctor, I hope you understand that, even if I had the money you're asking for, I would not buy your painting. There is no need to unwrap it. Believe me: I am glad you both survived the war. But you have been deemed useful in this new society of ours; your painting has not. To deal in Kozu is to deal in damnation. Yes, the war is over, but now the hunt is on for its criminals.

Let us put that aside for the moment. We have something in common and this should be celebrated, especially during this time of differences. Like the Americans, you were right to believe I once dealt in the great Kozu's art. And even more so to believe that I knew more of him than what I told his would be captors. Will it surprise you to hear me say how once, when I was apprenticed to my grandfather's offices in Paris, I accompanied him and Soutine on what Kozu had said would be a little 'expedition'? They took me through the abattoirs around La Ruche. I can see them now. *Un plaisir pour les yeux*: Kozu in some peacock print shirt he had sewn himself; Soutine in that jacket of his, like a boiler-suit cut off at the waist, wearing his only pair of shoes.

Down an alley, its cobbles and walls shining with drizzle, we came across a knacker, his arms posed, wielding a lump hammer: a stroke away from putting an old Lipizzan horse to its passing. A hessian sack covered the beast's face; its ears poked out through holes cut into the top. Holding onto the halter was the man's handsome daughter, her eyes large and keen. Kozu – perhaps sensing my disquiet, perhaps aroused by the look on the girl's face – approached the man. The knacker's heavy apron was white: the horse was to be his first job of the day. With Kozu whispering in his ear, the old fellow nodded his thick head, given shape by a bushy moustache and cropped hair, and passed the hammer over to the artist's hands. It took Kozu a single blow to split that horse's skull. Soutine, I remember, was sorely disappointed because the carcass was too heavy, too cumbersome, to transport back to the commune.

Surely, you have heard the rumours? And so you know just how vigilant was their study of anatomy. I wonder if the extremity of an action such as this passed over me as much when I was a younger man as it does now upon recollection? But then again, wasn't it Valery

who said, 'the skin is the deepest thing?' Kozu bragged
of the wonders those animals offered up. Raw textures
of colour, he said: mother-of-pearl tendons, cut slack
within an eviscerated rabbit; the flayed ox, split through
the ribs: so many muddied shades of white, against a
feast of rouge and brown. Soutine was the first to excel
at recording these spectacles on his canvases. But Kozu
advanced that art to another level altogether. And, yes,
that is why I must tell you about your painting, Doctor.
It deserves as much, as does Kozu himself. The moment
Macarthur landed at Atsugi Airport, our greatest artist's reputation crumbled. The Americans are looking
to hang him and the new generation of artists have,
like crows, hopped beyond the rubble of the past. Still,
I have no doubt, Doctor, that, much like myself, you
have the utmost respect for such adventurous types:
the Chaim Soutines and Yuichiro Kozus of the world.

Does it surprise you, I wonder, that I know which
work you have brought me from the parcel's proportions
alone? Let me describe for you the tableau: its Japanese
soldier, centre left, little more than a silhouette is bursting
into a darkened room. At his feet lies a white imperialist.
Was this Frenchman cut down by the soldier's bayonet
– that slash of gold, glittering in the doorway's bar of
honeyed light? We do not know. There is no blood on
the blade. Just real gold leaf flashing over muted oils.

The night Kozu put his last touches to your painting, Doctor, Wagner was playing on the gramophone. The grand march from the German's *Tannhäuser* – a favourite of Van Gogh. An hour past dusk and there Kozu was: studying his three models, pouring his soul into the forms he recast on his canvas. He closed his eyes often, cursed, remembering the scene the hour before, recalling the slant of a shadow on the soldier's collar, his neck, beneath the ear, the quality of brightness along the shadow's edge. How he wished he could freeze time, the sun's quick descent. That is why he chose gold leaf for the blade. It shone with a light beyond the shades he mixed, his highlights. He did not like to paint from memory. If the essence of *kokutai* was to be evoked, ordinary light would not do. Kozu said as much himself. The *body-national* needed a touch of the divine. His soldier was a saviour. A liberator. And, while we contemplate his valiant pose, our eyes are drawn to the shadows, past the fine European furniture (edges and grooves picked out with great care – the texture of heavy curtains), to the figure in the bottom right-hand corner. Her skin is dark, eyes narrow, the girl, who, almost invisible in her black smock, is sitting on her knees, hands tied behind her back. *What atrocity has been averted here?* we ask.

A week. That is all it took Kozu to render what in times gone by some of us might have called a masterpiece. No other documentary artist could work so quickly. Not with such grace and dexterity. It is no wonder the Army sent Kozu everywhere to record their greatest moments: the storming of Singapore, Hong Kong. Some have said he flew in the back of a torpedo bomber at Pearl Harbour. In March of 1945, he was stationed in Saigon.

Doctor, you must have graduated in the last wave of students to leave medical school during the war. You look so young. Indulge me. There are some facts about your painting you may not be aware of, or were too busy to pay much attention to, given the calamities that befell Tokyo the last year of the war. I do not mean to give a history lesson, to patronise a bright fellow like yourself, but you may find it difficult to picture our military policy in Indochina, what with our decisiveness elsewhere. The key term the diplomats used was the 'maintenance of tranquillity.' *The golden rule.* Allow the French legislative organizations to remain, we thought, leave the police, economy, education, and all other domestic affairs under French control. We were engaged elsewhere and Paris had fallen. Why disrupt a vital rest stop; why poison your well, your breadbasket? Major General Sumita, I heard, advised his staff to conduct negotiations in a dedicatedly peaceful and friendly way. But it was an uneasy status quo. The Army said it would not support the independence movements in our area of operations, but it did – except of course, the Communists. Many of our native supporters were disposed of by the French Sûreté. We said we would not create bases for operations against southern China (the French feared igniting Chinese interest in their stricken colony), but again we did, especially after the declaration of war on America and Great Britain, when the army surrounded the French administrative headquarters and stated that General Decoux would facilitate our military presence in any way we saw fit. The French had no choice but to agree. The fear of losing their colony altogether was just too great. And as for the independence of the peoples of Indochina? Our diplomats thought that a matter of importance, but only as a future concern. Such a standoff, of course, did not last.

And, I can tell you Doctor, Kozu's models were not Japanese, or French, as you may have heard elsewhere. All of them were Indochinese, even the gentleman on the floor, though he referred to himself as Chinese, despite having been raised under the same sulphorous sun. *Ces messieurs*, Doctor. *Those gentlemen*. That is how Kozu referred to your soldier and dead Frenchman. But is such a detail really worthy of note? After all, we all know Kozu's reputation, his predilection for the grandiose. Just take the story about the Russian tank, the one he drove himself into the quietude of the garden of his Tokyo studio so he might render it in a dramatic scene of his own making.

One could be forgiven for thinking the soldier in your painting Japanese. How his face almost fits. He was called Trau, an ugly name for a beautiful youth. It meant *ox* and was given him by his grandmother to ward off evil spirits. To Kozu, he looked like the boy leading the elephant on the back of the 100 piastre note. Just talking to you Doctor, brings to mind a vision of Trau, standing there, in that corporal's uniform , its white armband marked with a rising sun, imprinted with the character *An* – a military pun, meaning both *security* and *An*-nam, the middle kingdom of Vietnam. 'Painting from life is the path away from melancholy.' That is something the boy liked to say.

I realize I am ahead of myself. Permit me to slow down. Can I offer you the same bowl of millet and yams my wife served to the Americans? It is rough food, Doctor, especially for a man of your standing, though I do like to think the sweet flavour of the yam, its delicate orange colour, is imbued with a sort of rustic charm. After all, we have little else.

While we eat perhaps I should tell you about how I came to arrive at this point in my life – so ungrateful as I am for what I once, and I admit it, would have snapped your hand off for. No mere anecdote is required this time, but what I have heard the Americans call the 'cold hard facts'. I came to the Cape St. Jacques in the rain: rough waters made pleasant by quiet skies. No American aircraft could prowl the coast, you see. By midnight, the stars and insects came out. The drive into Saigon was long. At The Institute of the Southern Ocean, the Japanese economic school on the Gallieni Boulevard, two military policemen were waiting for me. With no time to unpack my things, I was taken to the Majestic Hotel, a billet for the Japanese military.

Major Honma's first words to me were, 'Look at the legs of the British officers!' I could see little of him, as I sat down at his rooftop table. His back was to the tropical sun. His shadow extended over the white table, the photograph of the English officers and their spindly legs. Limbs he was so bent on discussing. The Riviere de Saigon blazed, stretching both north and south, like wings sprouting from Honma's thick shoulders. Curving out of sight in either direction, those waters gave the impression of forming an enormous circle, a River of Life, as envisioned in Buddhist scripture and the *nihonga* paintings of Yokoyama Taikan, a favourite of my grandfather's. The sun was a hot coal. I thought, here was a man touched by the theatrical. Backlit as such, Honma could have been a vision of the Emperor himself, the faceless centre of our nation's flag. The *Hinomaru* personified.

Honma insisted, 'See?'

I did not *see* and nodded in agreement. Honma was a major in the Kenpeitai, Doctor. He could arrest anyone. Anyone at all. Even military officers up to four ranks above his own station. Imperial justice was his to interpret. I was not untouchable. Even today, many of his kind are unaccounted for by the British I hear, and the Americans, and the Dutch. All this trouble over a painting. The news clipping beneath his finger was from the Asahi Newspaper and showed General Percival on the day the British surrendered Singapore. I had seen the photograph before – had advised the cultural bureau to commission the documentary artist, Saburou Miyamoto to set the occasion in oils. But that was back in 1942. Things were not going so well.

'How spindly their legs are,' he said. 'And their knees. They're too thin. Those are weak joints, Takayanagi. I know about such things.'

'The joints look frail.'

'*Soh, soh,* They are *frail*. And spindly, like a spider crab's: that is how Kozu described them when I showed him this same picture.'

'Kozu is a genius.'

'He is from Hokkaido. He must have grown up

surrounded by the spiky bastards – the crabs that is, not the British. Though, I do question his attachment to the French. I've heard that you lived in France, too, Takayanagi.'

I told him I had.

Honma took a drag on his cigarette, which he held between his ring and baby fingers. An odd pose. An affectation. One I had seen perfected by a member of the Royal Family in the Philippines. He was a man who would never humble himself by supping on a bowl of millet soup. The cloud of blue smoke the major blew out over the stone railing beside him wheeled in the wet air above the rue Catinat, where it refused to dissipate.

At last he said, 'You are on intimate terms with Yuichiro Kozu, Takayanagi, are you not?'

'My grandfather represented his interests for many years in Tokyo, at the Midori Gallery on the Ginza. I met him in Paris. I wouldn't say we know each other well.'

'But you have been sent to Saigon to escort him back to the homeland. He and his military commissions. The Imperial Household itself has sent you.'

I was not to talk of such matters, but that meant nothing to a man like Honma. It was safer to bow, to nod, to say, 'Yes, Major Honma.'

'Let us understand each other, Takayanagi. Never would I dream of standing in the way of the Imperial Household, any more than I would with general headquarters. The Army sent Kozu here. Under my protection, he ventured north and painted the southern China front. The logistical preparations –to transport so valuable a consignment of national treasures back to Japan– are already made. Most of those paintings were completed in Hanoi. In fact, those paintings are at this moment on their way to the Cape St Jacques to be loaded onto the same hospital ship, which delivered you safely to my corner of the Empire. He tells me that all he has to do is finish a commission for Ambassador Yoshizawa.'

Bowing, I mumbled my apologies. I thanked Honma for his loyal service to the Emperor.

'Forgive me, but I have a humble request to ask of you Takayanagi. To my good fortune, Kozu has agreed to produce a painting for me. It is not to be anything spectacular; I can't really call it a commission, my rank does not really permit such privileges. He assures me he will start it very soon. He is very specific about the conditions. A true man of detail.'

Honma, I realised, did not want Kozu to return, according to my schedule. I thought a moment and then told the major how I had also been tasked with preparing, for want of a better term, a *safe house* for any valuable artworks in the city. Those in need of protection should the French revolt, or the Americans invade by sea. I had a list of such pieces, prepared in advance by a cooperative French administer, no doubt one of Honma's network. If the major could help me out in such matters, I would be most grateful. I assured him the works would take a little time to assemble – perhaps a week.

'So we have an understanding, then,' he said. 'I am sure I have some information about the colonial residences in Laithiau that may interest you.'

Not a word that I am telling you embellishes my connection to Kozu, Doctor, and yet how removed from him I have come to be. In truth, those first few days in Saigon were a blur, but, though I seem to meander, there is good reason to do so. Be assured I will make all clear in time.

I finally met Kozu in person three days after Honma's summons. At the time, we had not seen each other for fifteen years. I was called up from the crypt of the l'gélise Saint François-Xavier, the Roman Catholic church of Cholon, the Bastille of the Chinese City, and into the white heat of the street. A jade-coloured Adler limousine idled outside the gates, its rear engine augmented by some strange contraption for burning woodchips. Kozu was standing beside its open door, wearing something similar to a lieutenant-colonel's uniform. He had made it himself. Replete with extra leather belts and pouches, pleats and creases, he could have been wearing a painting by Braque. Perspiration stained my shirt and trousers, a white so dark it was yellow.

I approached him and he stared at me, eyes roaming over my face, my body, as a glutinous man moves between the dishes of a large meal. 'You!' he called out. 'So it is *you* they have sent to fetch me back to Tokyo – I was hoping for your grandfather.'

After apologizing for not contacting him earlier, I told the artist how busy I had been since my arrival.

'Busy? What, in there?' He looked at my escorts, two tired looking veterans, who seemed to be contemplating the stillness of a fly on the other side of the courtyard. I smiled as best I could, unwilling to risk his reaction, his flamboyant personality, with the knowledge that beneath our feet, in an second room dug into the crypt's lowest vault by a team of British prisoners, were stored canvases by the likes of Courbet, Matisse, Seurat, Carot. He did not pursue the issue.

'You must come by my studio, Takayanagi-kun.' He smiled. 'If you are anything like your grandfather, you will enjoy a little adventure. I'll wait for you on the corner of the rue des Marins.'

At three o'clock, I found his café. From underneath his cap, the artist pretended to snore, wake with a start, only to declare with a flourish, 'I have sent the car away.' A native waitress laughed at his antics, until she caught my expression. 'A walk will do you good. It is not healthy to spend so much time down a crypt. Believe me, I know.'

Doctor, the walk was a marvel in itself. I had only travelled by car between my lodgings at the economic school, the church and various houses in the French Quarter, where I gained entry with help from Honma's men. The major had insisted I not wander about. The Saigon Sûreté still policed the city.

Now, on foot, those strange streets came alive, their shabbiness worthy of Van Gogh's heavy brush strokes, the colours of lime, coriander, frangipani. Frying pork skin, mixed with brown sugar and garlic. Under the shade of kapok trees, invisible smoke dyed the air. Women ground peanuts. Everywhere locals in black smocks watched us through averted eyes. If we came close to them, they bowed, no doubt in supplication to Kozu's uniform. Only in our wake, did their voices sing out again, like birds settling after a fright.

We crossed the Arroyo Chinois and minutes

later the Canal dedoublement, where I watched the sunlight flash across brown water, slithers of space caught between brown boats, poled by brown skinned natives. To me, the canals looked to be full of flotsam, the debris of some great typhoon, which had flooded the city's busiest boulevards with stinking water.

Dusk dropped over the Chinese City. Blackout regulations kept the canal and its warehouses in darkness. We made slow progress along the route de Binh Bông, passing peasants heading back to their hamlets beyond the city limits. In their black pyjamas and against the white glow of the road's dirt, they resembled spent matchsticks. To our left the paddy fields and marshes of the countryside washed up against the dyke, a humming thundercloud of bullfrog songs.

We arrived at Kozu's villa in the dark. The artist pulled on a bell-chain and turned to me.

'I could not tell you earlier, but I am not ready to return to Japan, not yet,' he said.

Caught off guard, I spluttered something about the Americans. The fear of an invasion. The likelihood of French treachery.

'No. Not yet.'

'Is this because of Major Honma?' I asked.

'What's Honma to do with anything?'

The door opened and an old maid let us in. Her face,

I saw in the light of the taper-lamp she handed Kozu, was marked by some childhood disease. She greeted the artist, as though he were the house's returning patriarch.

Electricity was rationed. The studio of a war artist, no matter his reputation, did not warrant special attention. Darkness welled in the house, its high-ceilings, and somewhere within that vacuum, a gramophone played a waltz. I followed Kozu and his lamp. At his ease, the artist led me through the hall, past a tiger skin, then a pair of enormous elephant tusks set in a bronze stand. The flame moved like a cat's eye, across the burnished surface. The walls of the corridors were painted with writhing vines, a queer throwback to Art Nouveau, which extended as far as the ironwork of the spiral staircase we ascended.

We came to the door of a large bedroom. Inside, a veranda was visible through a set of tall bay windows. The same moonlight that cut its iron fencing into parallel streaks broke into a thousand fist-sized diamonds, scattering across the boards of the room's floor. The latticed panels of the house's outer wall were a sign the architect had surrendered to the climate at least once. The diamonds illuminated a large canvas laid flat on the floor: a true Asian, Kozu had long since abandoned the easel. The strange light created the illusion that the canvas was hovering. Within that frame I could make out little actual painting, just a large empty space, like the vacuous mists of a silk scroll. Kozu asked that I wait in the doorway. By then, the gramophone ground out a cyclical white noise somewhere by the open window.

The artist crept around the edge of the room, lifted the needle from the record and drew the blackout curtains, all the time muttering under his breath. After that he lit various candles around the room using his lamp's flame, his movements quick and practiced as if laying down strokes of paint. The details of the canvas consolidated, but there was not much to see, just a layer of burnt sienna under-paint. I stepped into the room and took a closer look. A figure, in rough outline, a graphite rifle held out before him, was charging into the blank, muddied space. A wispy set of lines picked out a doorway around him.

In short, it was your painting, Doctor; only, it wasn't a *painting* then. Just a thatch of pencil hatchings.

And then I saw them: a man in uniform; next to him another, his face covered by a bed sheet. I rushed around the edge of the canvas, grabbing Kozu by the arm. The artist, leaning over a bed that had been pushed over into the corner of the room, shook off my hand with irritation and returned his attention to a third figure, a girl dressed in the black pyjamas of a peasant. The girl roused and smiled at his touch, her teeth catching the lamplight. And what a beauty she was, Doctor. She rose from the bed, like a ghost, brushed the creases out of her simple clothing and ran her fingers through her long hair – a black mass that fell down to her waist, like a painting of a Heian courtesan.

'This is Kieu,' Kozu said. 'She is the lady of the house.' He gestured over his canvas to the two men lying on the floor. 'That there is Petrus, her husband, under the sheet. The other –the boy– is her brother.'

'You mean the soldier is a native?'

'*Un.*'

My fright left me and was replaced with a deeper sense of fear. 'He is impersonating an Imperial soldier! If Honma found out, he'd be executed.'

Kozu asked Kieu to bring us a drink (and so here I will pause, just briefly, to ask if you, Doctor, would you like another drink yourself. No? I don't blame you. The story is always more compelling than a cup of wheat tea. Well, then I'll continue). Kozu added that that we would wait for her on the balcony. With his boot, he nudged the boy in the soldier's uniform and said in French, '*Oi*, my friend here wants to hang you.'

The figure groaned and reached for the gramophone needle, which Kozu took from his fingers. The soldier drifted back off to sleep.

'This wretch, Takayanagi-kun, is my protégée: Trau.' Kozu took a jug of water from the washstand and soaked the boy's face.

The boy spluttered and got to his knees, shaking his head, eyes wide with confusion. His fists were clenched. In that uniform, its stitching loose, cotton scuffed, he was a vision of impudent rage, like one of the old timers I had seen marching back to Shanghai from Nanjing, his pain held at bay by amphetamines. He looked from Kozu to me, a Japanese stranger, and took a series of deep breaths to calm himself.

'We thought you'd be back sooner, Yuichiro,' the boy gasped. 'When you didn't come, we had a smoke to pass the time.'

Kozu nodded. 'What about him?' He motioned to the prostrate form on the floor.

'You'd better not. Petrus was smoking your Golden Bats even before you left.'

The figure at our feet mumbled something in his native tongue: a series of disjunctive plucks on a *koto* string.

Trau's legs shook but he managed to get to his feet. Kozu led us out behind the blackout curtain and onto the veranda. The heat was there, too, even in the white flashes of moonlight reaching up from the canal beneath us and moving across the walls. A pleasant heat. A tangible mass that absorbed me, as I eased down onto the stylish butterfly chair Kozu had pushed over for me. Its metal frame was wet. Trau lit a cigarette and exhaled smoke as sweet as incense, offering one to Kozu. The artist explained to the boy that I was an art dealer from Tokyo, the grandson of a legend. Not a military man.

'March,' Trau said, falling back into a chair of his own, the neck and shoulders of his khaki uniform still black with water. 'This is the best time of year to stay in Cholon, M. Takayanagi. You chose a good time to visit. April will be here soon. The humidity will return. And the sun will lose its clarity. Every surface will dull.'

The girl returned. She poured out three drinks from a decanter and said something to Trau. He translated. The wine was made from tamarinds, he explained, a local brew to circumvent wartime restrictions. His sister was worried it might be too sweet for my liking. Kozu, I noticed, watched her every move. After she disappeared inside again, his eyes remained fixed on the edge of the blackout curtains. As if sensing my questions, the artist sipped from his glass and said, 'Tell him Trau.'

The boy tapped ash from his cigarette and asked whether I was intimate with the works of Van Gogh. Of course, I said.

'I am the Dutchman's reincarnated soul,' he said. Not a living a ghost, he insisted; he was not possessed. What moved within him was a force, an inextricable intuition, which held him *in situ between East and West*. Those were his words, Doctor. Like you, I almost laughed, only the boy's sincerity kept me civil. Trau told me of how he had attended the Lycée Chasseloup-Laubat in Saigon, before his grand adventure north to study under Joseph Inguimberty at the Ecole Des Beaux-Arts in Hanoi. His stay proved both disastrous and fruitful. Director Inguimberty suffered, what Trau named 'a crisis of line,' and turned on the boy from the south, stating that colour was the better way to portray the tropical atmosphere. Trau agreed, in part, but could not abandon his expressive lines. They were as fundamental to him as fish sauce, a root of the Asian tradition. Van Gogh had understood the importance of outlines. Where the wild Dutchman had painted the fields around Arles, touched as he was by the aesthetics of the Japanese woodprint, Trau looked to paint in the other direction: an Oriental looking upon the paddy fields of his homeland with an eye to capture their essence in bright oils.

It was only to be expected that such an impressionable youth follow Kozu, the only Asian painter to make his name in Paris: a master of the *real*, when the avant-garde paraded their abstractionist rhetoric. Kozu had shown the world that Asians could pierce the look of the contingent world. That, for us, abstraction was nothing new. To the likes of Trau and Kozu, the very act of divorcing art from its mimetic function was a tyranny.

The story told, I emptied my third glass and poured myself another, by then feeling quite at home. 'If only we had some absinthe.' I said, quite outside of myself as I saluted the young corporal. 'And a couple of 2 franc whores.'

The young Viet smiled his 100 piastre smile. 'If only . . . But we do have Golden Bat cigarettes. Would you care for a smoke, M.Takayanagi?'

That night I learned about how Kozu came to be at the villa on the edge of the Chinese City, about how the master artist, on returning from a lecture he had given to the Anamese Royal Family in Hue, had come across the boy on the side of the road, where he stood, waist deep in mud, sketching a sleeping water buffalo in charcoal. When Kozu had quizzed the boy, he found out the youth had walked to the ancient capital and was heading back to Cholon. He had little more than ten piastres on him, much like Van Gogh had had when he walked out of Paris to Courrières and slept in a haystack, a hoar frost blanching the landscape around him. Apparently, on returning to Saigon, Trau had sent Kozu a portrait of the artist he had painted, an inversion of how Van Gogh introduced himself to Gauguin. Before you ask, Doctor, no; I never saw such a painting. Kozu had in turn, invited Trau to model for him, to take the role of the soldier in his commission for the ambassador.

The boy's French was excellent, his manner patient. I took his sweet tasting cigarettes and listened to his explanation of how his-brother-in-law was a rice merchant, the son of a radical Chinese father who had come to Cholon to make his fortune. That was how, out of custom with the all the other Chinese who occupied the canal district, Petrus had been named after a famous Saigonese dignitary.

Trau had come to live with his sister and her husband, after he returned home from Hanoi to find that his town had become, what he called, 'busy' with Communist cadres. Before the war, the village had been markedly different. Most of its houses were built of brick and not thatch. One family owned a generator, another, a French bicycle. Trau was very proud of his paternal village. It was a fount of civilization, where cactus fences were a thing of the past; where Nice tiles covered the hard-earth floors. Still, the villagers attended their ancestor's graves and grew their jack-fruit trees on the outskirts, for fear of the ghosts the fruits attracted. The villagers were exceptionally filial people, he disclosed with a shy smile. Then came Kieu and Petrus' marriage; the result of a defaulted loan.

We breakfasted in the garden next morning, rising in an hour of coolness after rain. The sky brightened quickly, but the sun took its time in reaching us, due the great height of the rice mill that stretched out from the mansion's eastern walls. High over our heads, to the west, was the chimney of Petrus' distillery. The villa, too, was impressive, a red-brick affair, more architecturally at ease on the rue de Recluse, under the shadow of the Eiffel Tower, than on the edge of the Canal *dedoublement*. The mill and distillery were alive with voices, as was the canal itself. On its far side, we watched a group of POWs shift crates from a barge onto a truck, under the eye of a Korean soldier with a strong accent, a sight I had grown accustomed to in Shanghai and whilst working under the Catholic church in Cholon.

'They blew up the prison camp last month,' Kozu told me, 'their own bombers. Can you believe that?'

But I was only half listening. The delights laid out on the table before us by the ugly maid amazed me more. Somehow Petrus had access to coffee and cow's milk and other luxuries not even the French administrators could get their hands on. His wealth was truly formidable; the war could not erode it. Quite the opposite. With oil at a premium, Petrus was augmenting his fortune through the distillation of aviation fuel from his rice stocks and dismissed any mention of the famine in the north.

As we ate, Trau painted his ekphrastic dreams for my benefit. Lost amongst his own words, Doctor, he reminded me very much of my own grandfather, back at our gallery on the Ginza.

'I intend the marriage of two shades of green,' he said between bites of rice-flour-bread, 'not mixed colours; not a single shade; but two antonymous colours, placed side by side on a canvas. The outcome will be a kind of magic. One could call it the mystic vibrations of kindred tones.' Where Van Gogh obsessed over yellow, Trau loved green.

Kozu refused to eat, complaining that the opium-laced Golden Bat cigarettes had given him stomach cramps. He chose, instead, to walk up and down the edge of the canal, watching those prisoners, occasionally coming back to the table to pause and watch Trau's sister, as she listened to her brother swear an oath that he would not rest from painting the rice fields and rubber plantations of his homeland, until he had succeeded in finding two such mates, had laid them down together as bedfellows, or better yet, as two tragic lovers in a tomb. The mutuality of their presence, he assured her and the whitening sky, would revive them both.

In all honesty, I was lost for words most of the time. How was I to react to the young Viet's manifesto? To derail the youngster's ideals would have meant angering Kozu. That, I was not prepared to do. Still, I wanted to say to him, 'You are Asian, boy! Why muddy that? Why not seek after something truly Asian, not diluted by a westerner's ravings?' Don't worry, Doctor; I recoil just as much on recalling that memory as you do on hearing it! Can you believe I thought such a thing? Of Van Gogh of all people? But alas I did. If it was not for Petrus I would have said to the young Viet that we Japanese were fighting a war to keep Asia for its own, sure to remind Trau that if the Kenpeitai were to hear him, they would charge him with sedition.

It was Petrus who gave voice to my doubts.

'What is there to like about the countryside?' He questioned from over his coffee cup. 'The cutthroats? The revolutionaries? Disease? The fields filled with centuries of shit?'

For the first time that morning, I heard Kieu speak. 'I like the rice fields,' she said, her French accent soft, as if she were from the Provence-Alpes-Côte d'Azur. 'The sky, the way it hangs on them – or, just before harvest, the passing of a breeze through the long green stalks: it reminds me of ripples crossing a temple pond.'

'Only at a distance,' Petrus countered. 'Up close, those stalks look more like the fur of a mangy dog. The smell is worse still. The route de Bing Bông is a tourniquet. The road keeps disease at bay.'

Kieu excused herself in her native tongue and joined Kozu at the water's edge. I watched them both, very much aware that, out of the corner of his eye, Petrus was watching me. How lightly the Viet girl walked, Doctor. How often she smiled, when talking with the old artist. I wondered what they could be speaking of. I can recall lamenting, in that moment, the fact that Kozu no longer painted women's portraits. After his first expeditions to the China front in '38, the military censors had deemed his Asian nudes decadent. 'Ours is a holy war,' one critic had written soon afterwards. 'Who would choose the bark of even the smoothest tree, if it meant neglecting its blossoms?'

During dinner on March 9th, a week after my arrival in Saigon, General Tsuchihashi, the commander of Japanese forces in Indochina, slipped away from a reception he was holding for a number of French diplomats and administrators, at his residence in the centre of Saigon. At 7.00 pm, the General issued his

French counterpart, General Decoux an ultimatum: secede Indochina, or face forced disarmament. Preparations had already been made, ammunition distributed. Decoux stalled for time. He was granted two hours. Not all Japanese units, on alert since the previous night, waited for the two hours to play out. They went on the offensive. Taking advantage of the pockets of chaos that followed, I accompanied Honma and his men, as they rounded up suspected members of the Free French, their sympathizers and *métis*, Eurasian members of the Sûreté. I took my list and annexed those artworks at greatest risk of damage if full scale insurrection were to erupt. We encountered little resistance. At around 9.00 pm, I remember, there was burst of automatic weapons fire, somewhere close to the military hospital, then silence.

It sounds extraordinary to tell you now, Doctor, but I had completed my work by late afternoon of the following day, Honma's men were so efficient. I returned to Cholon without sleeping, where I deposited the works I had liberated from the villas of the French Quarter, the Governor General's office and home in particular (one detachment of Honma's men even struck out for the Ville Blanche, the governor's residence on the coast). Japanese units were visible on the streets, their smiling young men (those who had never seen action before) a stark contrast to the weathered faces of their older colleagues, those who were supposed to be recuperating after action in Burma. Sound-trucks travelled the streets, sporting the flags and slogans of the Greater East Asia Co-Prosperity Sphere, passing under many billboards still carrying the images of Marshal Pétain. Local civilians stayed in their houses.

Once, during the night, and again at first light, the major dispatched runners to check on Kozu's so-called *Yellow House* in Cholon. A company of French soldiers had escaped the city via the route de Bing Bông during the night and faded into the paddies beyond. My work complete, I ensured the major I would go to the artist myself. The operation of the previous night seemed to have invigorated the major and he talked to me excitedly about some of the pieces I had acquired. Still he smoked his cigarettes in his affected manner, but his tone of voice had softened, so that I started to feel a sense of camaraderie well up between us.

'Tell Kozu, I now have sufficient materials to at least start on my painting,' the major said, as I took my leave. 'The artist should be moving onto other projects by now. You should both come out to the Hippodrome this afternoon.'

There it was, Doctor. An invitation I paid little attention to, seeing that I did not really follow the major's meaning. That invitation has landed me here, in this old house, living in fear of the Americans, of their interest in me and my grandfather's gallery, exiled as I am to these mountains, to a life of millet gruel and vegetables I pull from the soil with my bare hands. And the snows will settle here soon. What will I do then? Your painting is more dangerous to me than you can imagine. At the time, I gave little thought to the major's enigmatic words. I don't think I even questioned what he meant by *materials*. Honma was a major in the Kenpeitai, as I've already said. It was best to obey. It was safer. More settling.

I found Kozu asleep on the bed tucked away in his studio, but before I could rouse him, Trau shouted up from the foyer. The boy was almost dancing with happiness.

'We are free,' he gushed. 'The French have been swept aside! This is no longer *Indochine*, but a new country, an ancient one: welcome, M. Takayanagi, to *Vietnamien*.'

I asked after Petrus. A rich Chinaman like him was to be watched at such a delicate time. But Trau was too preoccupied to take my questions seriously. With great élan, he revealed to me his latest works, three paintings he had worked on throughout the night – one after the other, after the other– and into the morning. All three were of the countryside directly across from the villa, their paint wet and fields gouged out of chartreuse and pear green.

When Kozu came to, I informed him of Honma's message. He looked uncertain and out of cheer, Doctor. Quite out of character. Trau showed him those same three paintings of his, but the master artist was unable to say a single word of praise. He did not even grace the young Viet's efforts with a smile.

He said that he must hurry; that Trau must help him complete his portrait of the liberating soldier. What with the coup, the painting was of vital importance, more now than ever. While he mixed his paints and prepared his palette, he explained to both Trau and I that your tableau, Doctor, had been commissioned by the Army: that the grand image was to act as a means of justifying the military action that had swept the French from administrative power. It would be taken most probably to the Hotel de Ville. There, in that grand foyer it would proclaim our conquering army a force of liberation.

I saw through him. Honma, surely, was looking to collect on whatever agreement they had made. The major wanted his portrait completed. The privileges and freedoms granted Kozu by the major came with a price. Still, the master artist could not abandon your painting Doctor.

How long had I spent watching Kozu during my spare hours? How much longer still did I look on the artist's efforts to lift Trau and Petrus' forms from the mist of its burnt-sienna under paint, along with the walls and floors and furniture of the *Yellow House*? How long did Kozu agonize over Kieu's bound body? It is hard to say. There the canvas lay, *your* painting Doctor, on the floor of the studio, an expression of our struggle against western imperialism. Kozu was bent over Trau's figure, shuffling round the edge of the image so as to focus on the grain of a cabinet, all the time instructing the young Viet on where to work up an edge of curtain, a fold in his own painted uniform, a crease in his sister's smock. For that past week, the painting had been a symbol to me, grand and beautiful, but somehow strangely abstract. Overnight, its metaphors had turned to flesh.

Trau saw it too and quickly dropped the subject of his own paintings, those three brightly coloured and empty landscapes, which he left to dry on the balcony. Every word, every instruction Kozu issued the young Viet, looked to penetrate Trau to the core. He revelled in the oils that gradually coated his fingers, then the whole of his hands. At one point, Kozu ordered him to dress once again into his corporal's uniform, after which the artist ordered the boy to stand, to burst through the balcony window curtains, to pause, telling him to keep his back erect, legs slightly bent, face stern, proud. An hour later, his corporal's uniform dark with sweat in the late afternoon heat, Trau once again fell to his knees, taking up fresh brushes, and following Kozu instructions with renewed vigour.

Wagner blared in the background: the grand march from the German's *Tannhäuser*. That favourite of Van Gogh's.

Petrus, by that time had returned from whatever errand had taken him into the city. He came to the studio, looking for his wife. Kozu told him to take up his usual position at Trau's feet. The Chinaman refused. Kozu lost his temper and informed his host what would happen to him if he failed to cooperate. Once installed at Trau's feet, *en pose*, Petrus chain-smoked one Golden Bat cigarette after another, until his head finally slumped down onto the floorboards. Until that moment, Kozu kept me busy by barking orders at me. 'Open that tin of turpentine; wash out these brushes; open the curtains wider; fetch us a lamp, the light is fading too quickly; Trau needs a glass of water.' And the like. But with Petrus unconscious on the floor, Kozu's mood shifted.

'Fetch Kieu,' he said.

I found the girl in the garden, pacing the canal

bank, dressed in a cotton blouse – yes, it was yellow, with a mandarin neck. Her hair was up. What details to remember Doctor! I had grown so accustomed to watching her pose for Kozu in that black peasant's smock he had found her that I had forgotten she was the wife of the wealthy businessman. I informed her of Kozu's request, of how urgently she was needed.

'You are the body of Asia lost,' Kozu said to the girl in the studio as he bound her hands, his voice strained. 'Lost: then saved, by the heroic coming of we Japanese.'

Kozu and Trau painted well into the evening.

Perhaps the raid that levelled part of the Chinese City that night was in reprisal for our military's success – our last success, as it was to prove to be. A token, Doctor, a means to let us know we were surrounded. The bombers arced round into Saigon from the southeast. Kozu and I were sitting in the garden of the *Yellow House* when they came. A siren pierced the sky and a strange stillness fell over the garden, along the canal, and those tufts of jungle that crept up to the water's edge past the distillery, where the palms gazed down at their own reflections. The insects and frogs in the paddies fell silent, too. I stared at the black sheen covering the canal, that oily surface, whose darkness seemed to spread out from the filthy membrane to ooze over the boats and banks and leaves and walls and of the city.

The drone of heavy engines rose out from that silence, as if the planes were spectral, a plague of ghosts gathering for vengeance above the Plain of Reeds. I will reiterate Doctor: it was a night raid. An unusual tactic for the whites by that time in the war, seeing we no longer had any fighters with which to counter them. All of that fuel Petrus' plant distilled and none of it could save the city of his birth.

I believe I said to Kozu something about the locals, how I imagined them smiling up at the enemy aircraft with those vacant Asian smiles of theirs, neither happy, nor angry, but just because the foreigners were *there*, over their country. How could I have known that only two days before, on the eve of our great coup in Indochina, American bombers had dropped petroleum jelly and incendiaries on Tokyo; that they had turned the city to ash, my grandfather's gallery included? It would take weeks for such a truth to become known to me.

'You're drunk,' was the artist's reply.

'No more than you.'

On the other side of Arroyo Chinois, an anti-aircraft battery opened up. A melancholy sound. It all seemed so ridiculous, those shells bursting amongst the stars, bringing to mind thoughts of summer fireworks over the Sumida River back home. I told Kozu we should probably find a shelter. Did the house have a cellar? I was not too concerned at that point, believing as I did, that the planes would strike at the docks on the far eastern side of the city.

Kozu turned his shoulders and looked back into the house through the latticed wall. A dimmed lantern burned inside, on a bureau angled obliquely into a corner of the parlour, its orange ball made invisible to anyone on the other side of the canal. There Petrus sat, opium-dazed, writing what he called, 'an epic poem.' An hour had passed since the Chinaman stirred from his drugged sleep and found his wife kneeling before Kozu, her hands bound behind her back, smiling at the painter. On seeing Petrus awake, Kozu had backed away from his canvas and told Trau to change out of his uniform, to wash his hands. Whatever spell the girl cast over the artist when she modelled for him was broken. He would not lay down another stroke that night, he said. Besides he had decided that gold leaf was better for the bayonet of Trau's rifle. The process of digging down into his layers of paint, to strip away that slither of gunmetal and clean the oil off the canvas was too intricate a task to attempt at night. And where was he to lay his hands on such a precious material? There was no choice but to wait for daylight. Moreover, he was exhausted. The job of preparing and applying the bole was beyond him for the time being, whether he could find any gold or not. The adhesive, too, would take an age to dry enough to become sticky, for the gold to be applied.

The lantern cast shadows inside the Chinaman's hollow cheeks. Its light welled in the deep polish of the desk's mahogany, like something from Van Gogh's *Night Cafe*.

Kieu was somewhere in the parlour, close to her husband and out of sight of us. I could feel her presence. I could almost hear her breathe, or so I thought. Most probably she was right behind Kozu, a dark shape filling so few holes of the lattice work. But she was listening to every word we said, of that I was sure. Listening. Waiting for us to move to safety. Kozu was tense, but remained in his chair, as if he too felt the girl's eyes and ears. He wanted to impress her.

The sirens cried on. The air defences *putted* and *pom-pom'ed*. Every surface sweated. My clothes were damp, as always, and there was no hope of relief. The first bombs whistled down and exploded. From the veranda, I looked out through the trees of the garden and watched the amber glow of conflagration thicken amongst the warehouses to the east, then the north. The bombs were a good ways off, but, still, they fell on Cholon. This was not to be a raid on the Docks de Saigon, after all. Frantic voices erupted from the distillery's complex. The wood decking beneath my feet vibrated. Shocked into waves, the canal's surface lapped the pilings like netted fish.

Kieu slipped out of the darkness and stood beside us, her back to the canal. Her eyes were wide and bright against her dark face. Kozu stirred. His measured movements exuded confidence, his very silence inspiring calm.

We made our way through the parlour, Kozu leading Kieu by the elbow. Dipping his pen into the inkwell, Petrus refused to look up at us, to acknowledge our passing. Trau met us in the hall, fretting over the fate of Kozu's painting and not his own.

'It's still wet,' the boy said again and again. It was as much as we could do to stop him running up the stairwell and to the studio. 'Are you just going to abandon it?' he raged, but his sister calmed him.

Outside the rumble of the bombs became a roar. A strange wind whipped up and around us. The air quaked. I stumbled about because my legs were shaking and the ground heaved. I cursed the dyke and its road, the white gravel that was as good as a lit boulevard, a neon strip leading the bombers along the canal to the distillery. The earth swallowed us. A slit trench, Doctor, dug by the men of the distillery. Local voices babbled up and down that wrinkle in the earth. I tasted the damp soil on my lips.

A hundred yards away, a warehouse flew to splitters, then another behind it, in the opposite direction to the Yellow House. A barge on the canal exploded. Warm water fell on us like soft rain. White smoke, Doctor. The stink of cordite. All this I remember with vivid intensity. The flashes of light. Kozu, with his lips pressed into Kieu's hair. Shockwaves. Shrapnel – not quite splitting the air at that distance, but falling none the less.

Something struck me on the head, right on the crown, like a nut falling from a tree. I wondered what it could have been, where it had come from. Can you imagine, Doctor? The bombs were falling closer and closer and a strange curiosity took over me. Was its part of a rivet from the boat? Or the tip of a nail wrenched free from a roof beam? My fingers sifted through the soil in the bottom of the trench, around Kozu and Kieu's knees. And there I found *it*, Doctor. Human teeth. A fragment of a person's overbite.

Honma arrived the next morning and I accompanied the major on an inspection of the warehouses close to the distillery. The shock of having survived the attack was wet within my nerves, like the paint on Trau's canvases. I could not stop babbling.

'This reminds me of Ginza after the Earthquake of '23,' I said at one point. 'I recognize the stench. It's like rotten apricots.'

Kozu had already taken Kieu back to the villa, leaving Trau to wander through the debris, to stare at the coolies, gathered from the local warehouses, who were laying out the bodies of those killed in the raid. Military policemen paced up and down the route de Bing Bông, handkerchiefs wrapped around their faces. Over a megaphone a voice boomed out through the smoke. I asked Honma what it was saying.

'*Look at what the imperialists inflict upon your people*; that is what it says.'

The thought of those teeth kept coming back to me, their texture haunting my fingertips, as I played with their cloth bundle in my pocket. How fallible the body was. How easily something like a tooth, even a jaw, could be lost, blown loose by an explosion. It was not something I had thought much about before. Eyes, yes. And fingers.

I said as much to Honma, before adding, 'Perhaps, it is time I left for Japan. The ship is a week overdue. That alone is dangerous. People will ask questions. Besides, Major, with the utmost respect, it is too dangerous here for Kozu to remain here in Saigon.' I let the major mull over my proposal, refraining from pushing the point.

When we walked up to the iron gate of the Yellow House, Honma directed my line of sight to a faint ribbon of smoke lifting straight into the sky from the distillery's chimney. Already the place was operational.

'Don't you feel, Takayanagi,' he said, 'that it is a great coincidence that your Chinaman's works were spared last night? The power station over the canal was not so lucky.' He did not expect an answer, of that I am sure. If I had offered my opinion on the matter, he would have turned on me. With a tight-lipped smile the major passed by the gates, pausing only once to look up at the house's grand façade.

'Would you come in for some refreshment?' I asked.

Honma refused. 'There is a city to police.'

Doctor, you must be familiar with the saying, 'He can recite the morning prayer without learning it: the boy who lives before the temple gate.' I guess for most of my life I was that boy, living under my grandfather's watchful eye, the Midori my home-from-home, what with my father's continual absence.

To many people – my grandfather and his clients, alike – the gallery was a threshold, more the *house beside the temple gate* than the temple itself. There one could stand on the edge of the soot and muck of Tokyo, the restraints of business and fine living, and look upon Kozu's work. His enormous canvases, his Realist mode of illuminating the beauty of the Japanese woman, the care he gave to refining that particular shade of white that defines our beauties' skin, how it is haunted by an undercoat of pale blue, almost invisible to the eye, a ghostly quality quite unlike the pink bravado of Caucasian women. And the lustre of our women's hair: only Kozu could capture that tactility and amaze my grandfather's clients. Sometimes, I believe, my grandfather thought himself alone in his gallery, and not entertaining a wealthy patron, a member of the Matsui clan, or someone of equal standing. I can hear him now, his thoughts spoken aloud, as he wondered why Kozu chose to paint his women with their hair down and not worn up in their usual coiffeur.

Yes, Doctor, Kozu's works are as familiar to me as that temple prayer, lodged within my heart, my memory, though I never paid them much attention. It was only after my apprenticeship in the Paris offices that I took note of Kozu as a man, and only then, as an exhibitionist. What did he know of Soutine's suffering? I asked myself, after having watched him dispose of that horse. Still, his works, so fawned over by both the Paris and Tokyo elite, so praised by the critics and connoisseurs, did not leave their lasting impression until that day of the air raid. Only then did Kozu's depth as an artist become apparent to me.

I see I confuse you, Doctor. Permit me to reveal the true nature of Kozu's crimes, the motive behind the Americans' search, the reason why I cannot buy your painting. Ask yourself this Doctor, why are the OSS so insistent on collecting any works by the artist? Why those from Indochina, in particular? Why this picture you have brought me?

Whilst Honma was arranging for one of his trusted rickshaw drivers to return me to the economic school on the Gallieni Boulevard (many of our officers were weary of travelling by such a means of transport, Doctor, fearing French agents – but I can tell you, the opposite was true: many of those men, their limbs dark and thin like willow branches, were under the employment of the Kenpeitai!), Kozu appeared at the gates of his Yellow House. Until that moment, I had never actually seen the two men together, though each man had spoken so much of the other that I felt a bond of brotherhood between all three of us.

To my surprise, Honma simply gave a curt bow, more in deference to Kozu's rank than as a mark of respect to the artist, to a man of intangible worth. Or so it seemed to me at the time.

Kozu told the major that he would accompany me to my billet. Honma grunted his agreement. No mention was made of the painting Kozu was supposed to be creating for the Kenpeitai officer; that was, until our rickshaw was about to pull away. At that moment, Honma leaned into the cab and said in a low voice, 'Hold on to this fellow, Kozu-sensei. (By which he indicated the rickshaw driver.) He'll take you to where you need to go. I'm sure Takayanagi here won't mind. Actually, he'll rather enjoy the distraction I think, what with the events of last night.'

At the school, I changed out of my filthy clothes and washed the night's dirt and soot from my skin, my finger nails. There was no running water; just a large earthen pot, used to collect rainwater. Standing there, naked, dipping a bowl into the tepid water and pouring it over my skin, I felt wretched, like a native. The luxuries of Petrus' villa were a dream from another world. I longed for the cleansing waters of a hot spring, to go home, to feel the chill of real March air, whilst bathing in an outside pool at my favourite spa resort in the Yatsugatake Mountains, indeed, not far from here, Doctor. If I had only known what would happen after the war. Even the conditions at the school, Spartan as they were, were better than this farmhouse, these tattered mats and millet gruel.

Kozu, after a quick discourse with the school's rector on the state of the war, joined me in my room. I showed him my trophy, those four teeth that had struck me on the head and which I had, by then, wrapped in cotton wool, having decided to keep them safe in a glass jar I had removed from one of the school's laboratories. To this day I don't understand why I did that, Doctor – why I kept such a grizzly reminder of my fear, why I showed them to the artist. Perhaps a man like you can empathise with such a brutal act.

The artist turned the jar over in his hands and sighed. 'I tried to sleep this morning. But the sound of the bombs echoed in my ears – that whistle of theirs in particular. I just couldn't shake the fatigue. I feel it now. It fills me like water.'

I told Kozu what I had told Honma; how I thought Cholon wasn't safe; how the whole of Indochina would fall with an American amphibious invasion within weeks. His painting of Trau, of his liberating warrior, could be left. I recommended to Kozu that he return with me to the homeland. The hospital ship would not hold on much longer.

'I cannot. Honma will not allow it. Besides, I must paint his damned portrait.'

What he said to me next, Doctor, has haunted me ever since: 'I know this war is already lost. That is why

I must paint what Honma wants me to. I must show the horror of it all. If I do not, I am doomed.'

I reassured him that the Imperial House would not permit the military police to harm him, at which he smiled.

'It is not Honma that scares me.'

I pressed him for an explanation, but he just smiled.

Putting down the jar on my cot, he stood up. 'You heard the major. Our rickshaw awaits. We can't keep the major waiting.'

Doctor, I do not wish to dwell on the nature of the establishment to which we were delivered, but, to be brief, it was a *green house*, one of the brothels run by the Kenpeitai to garner favours and information from its clients. Honma was waiting for us in a back room, his face and neck a livid red hue. A ceiling fan cut the air above us, stirring up the heat and heavy pall of opium. The major was in good spirits, offering us whiskey, which neither Kozu or I refused.

'Have you ever been to Kure, Takayanagi?' Honma asked after he had poured out our drinks. 'Unlike the two of you, I have never been to Manchuria. My previous posting was in Java, but I assure you, Takayanagi, the morning I disembarked from that port, the cold was intense. I don't think I had ever felt such a chill in Japan before and to think, that was the last time I saw our homeland. The scene was remarkable. Black cliffs fell into black water and great mists rolled down from the mountain peaks, surrounding the port on all sides. You couldn't see the warehouses clearly, or workshops, or the dock cranes, for that matter. But I tell you what we could see: standing on deck, we could make out the carrier Amagi, moored out a little ways in the bay. Gentlemen, I tell you, the way the cloud cover floated above the sea, breaking up the shape of that great ship, I was speechless. I do not have your expertise, but I tell you her steel hull, it was storm blue, like a *hanwei* spearhead.'

The major refilled our glasses.

'*Amagi*. Educated men like you must be familiar with the Chinese characters of the ship's name? They mean, "castle in the sky." In that moment, I thought of how little of our glorious country I had seen with my own eyes. I have never ventured north, not to your home Kozu-sensei, to Hokkaido, or to Aomori, to the Amagi Pass, after which the carrier was named. How insignificant I felt looking out at that ship, at the great beauty of that port in winter, between the sea and the mountaintops. The great sublimity of our land touched me.'

Kozu shifted in his seat. Though he tried to camouflage his feelings, I could sense he wanted the major to get to the point, to explain what we were doing in there. The major, already drunk on whiskey, was now intoxicated with nostalgia. 'To think, Takayanagi, I had seen Kozu-sensei's *The Shoukaku Departs Kure* at the Holy War Exhibition in '43. I thought it a fine painting then, but after seeing the Amagi with my own eyes, I felt as though I were seeing the painting again, afresh as if Kozu's hand was rendering the port, the great ship, as I looked on. I remembered what one of my friends had told me once, about how, at a private viewing of Kozu-sensei's works at the Imperial Palace the whole of the general staff saw a figure in one of your paintings move. Seeing the Amagi, my heart was stirred with great pride.

'You flatter me too much, Major Honma,' said Kozu.

'No, no. Quite the opposite. I cannot praise you enough. That is why I am so honoured by your agreement to paint my portrait.'

A chill went through me. I expected the major to stall, to explain how he would not let Kozu return to the homeland, not until his portrait was complete.

Kozu said, 'And I do not see why we don't get started as soon as possible. The air raid has brought to the surface many unsavoury things.'

Honma nodded. 'Yes. Don't think that your Chinaman's good fortune last night went unobserved.

How convenient that, while the rest of the canal area was hit hard, the power station especially, his whole complex was left unscathed. His distillery was completely left intact. What providence.' The major's eyes, wet with drink, glistened. 'So, I have decided to arrest him.'

'A wise decision, Major.' Kozu poured Honma another finger. 'This may be the very opportunity we discussed the other day – when we spoke at the racetrack. Though I must say I am not without reservations. I feel it my duty to say that leaving a man's wife to fend for herself is a great shame. It will be dangerous for a woman to live alone in that house. Not in Cholon, not with the marshes so close. As such, I would be glad if you decided to remove her into my custody.'

Honma's smile grew, but he agreed, adding that Kozu should come by the racetrack the next day. Time was of the essence. Once again, the major made reference to the great preparations he had made, so that his portrait could be completed. You are quite right, Doctor. This time my interest was pricked. I asked the same questions as you: what preparations? What materials? Why would Kozu have to drive all the way up to the north of the city for a commission? Why couldn't the major come by the villa, to the studio Kozu had already established? Only, I dared not voice my concerns.

The major continued, addressing me directly. 'Soon, Takayanagi, Kozu-sensei here will have finished his work for me, if his reputation for speed is anything to go by. Then you can whisk him off to Tokyo, but before you do, you too should come by the racetrack. I'm sure it will be quite the experience for a civilian, such as yourself. Feel free to enjoy the establishment, gentlemen. I feel I must be fully rested for our big day tomorrow. And as for your repository at the church, Takayanagi, your so-called *safe house*, I have taken measures to ensure the artworks there remain safe. I took care of the matter personally. Not a soul is left who knows of the secrets buried in the crypt, other than you and I, and the guards I personally selected to protect you. I assure you, the church will be quite safe. Quiet.'

Kozu gave me a knowing look and poured us all another drink.

Of course, Doctor, I was horrified. Never did I think that the men Honma had provided me with would meet such an end. And that was just the beginning. Remember those *preparations* I made mention of moment ago? Their true nature I will make clear soon enough.

Frequent squalls darkened the sky the next day. The rain in the morning was black with ash, but by the afternoon, the windows of the villa were washed clean. Kozu and I were taken to the Saigon Hippodrome in Honma's Adler. It was during that ride that the major explained his plans, as the artist and I listened to his discourse on sword technique. There was to be an execution and Honma had already formed his opinions on the best angle Kozu should view the beheading from, how close the artist could stand. The tales we may have heard from old army hands, of gushing blood and the like, were an exaggeration, he assured us. As proof, the major said he would not remove his white gloves.

It took an age for our car to work its way through the network of streets and canals, passing the Chinese Pagoda on the rue de Cay Mai on the way. By the time we arrived at the Hippodrome to the west of Saigon and north of Cholon, the afternoon was all but spent.

To call the place a race track was an exaggeration. It was little more than a stretch of flat land, the track roughly cut from the grass by the stamp of horses' hooves, the edges of which were marked by a barb-wire perimeter. The Korean guard who opened the barrier had a bruised face, a closed-over right eye. According to my driver, not a single race had run since the Imperial Army came to Saigon. Still, the grass would not grow back. Spread out across the course's central expanse was a series of tents, as if a garrison were billeted there.

On leaving the car, I was overcome by a smell similar to the one I told you of earlier, of the abattoir. When the stench of overripe apricots gets in your nose it will not come out. But this was even darker. Older. Clouds of flies blackened the air. Honma said that there was still some time before the prisoners would arrive. The Chinese Chamber of Commerce Building, the Kenpeitai's central jail, was even further away than the villa.

'I expect, Kozu-sensei that you wish to continue with your sketches?' Honma said. 'I have arranged things as you asked them to be left.'

A shallow bow and the major paced off to the far side of the compound. Kozu waited until Honma had disappeared into a tent, before saying, 'Well then Takayanagi-kun, welcome to the realm of hungry ghosts.' He did not look up to meet my eyes. His hand rested on the flap of the nearest tent. 'Let me show you something.'

Lifting the flap to, he asked that I follow him inside. That is how I discovered the true purpose of the tents; that they were there for a reason. Not to billet troops, Doctor, as they appeared to do from outside the wire. No. What I saw inside haunts me to this day. Lines of bodies, Doctor. Those soldiers killed on the night of the coup, or in the air raid, I did not know. Some were Frenchman, others Japanese, though only by their uniforms could I tell them apart in some cases. They were laid out on raised cots. I have not the words to express the scene, Doctor. Magritte, perhaps, could see the sense in it. But only Kozu's eye could do it justice.

Kozu began to walk amongst the litters. Many of the bodies had swollen and blackened with the heat, their heads looking like overripe grapes. The swelling face of one soldier had bent the frames of his spectacles out of shape. His lips belonged to a Negro caricature, not an Imperial soldier.

'When I listened to Lieutenant-General Saikai address our troops after the taking of Hong Kong, I heard him call this is a war between races. That when we kill the enemy we are avengers, easing the brooding anger within us, within Asia.' Kozu pointed to the line of litters. 'Look at these two: one without an arm, the other a leg. How tranquil they look.' (I, for one Doctor, could see only dead flesh.) 'Tranquillity is the absence of emotion. Somebody said that. Don't you think they whisper to us? Don't they say, *to be whole is good*?'

'I still don't understand.'

'Petrus is to be the star attraction of our little show.' The artist's words trailed off. He paced the grid once more, following a column of litters for five or six paces, then a row for two and then changing direction again.

'The rules have changed, Takayanagi-kun. Before, when I painted the rot of the battlefield, my paintings disappeared. The Imperial dead, or at least their images, were not to be exhibited in public. Now the Americans are coming – not just to here, but to the homeland. Now we are asked to depict our fallen, to bind our people, the *kokutai*, together. We are to be one in our anger and suffering. Honma wants a *memento mori* of his own, a testament to his power over life and death. I agreed to paint an execution for him, only he didn't want a formal situation. What he wants is for me to fabricate a battle around him, so it will look like he is performing an action in battle: retaliation, justice. This,' Kozu motioned to the dead, 'is all part of his preparations. As you can see, they are extravagant. He offered to have the bodies taken outside if I desired; to lay them out as if in some diorama. The Americans are coming, Takayanagi-kun. What will you tell them about today? About what you have stored under that church in Cholon? Will I doom myself, knowing the Americans will not stand for such scenes, for such uses of art? Never. I will paint the horror so vividly, as to state that I was witness to the brutality of the Imperial Army. I will say that I, Yuichiro Kozu, recorded what

I saw on purpose, with the utmost care. Here is my proof. My paintings are records, documentation of my horror. They will have to let me go. They will probably think me a hero.'

Close to dusk, Petrus' transport arrived and the Chinaman, along with five others – three of whom looked French – were dragged down from the truck. Their legs hung limp, their knees banged against the tailgate, but Petrus for one seemed beyond caring. He and his compatriots were taken out into the expanse of grass in the middle of the racecourse, to what resembled a parade square, a shielded spot, what with the dim light, the distance from the perimeter, the lines of tents. Nobody outside the compound would able to see what was going on. Honma was careful that way. He liked to keep about him the mystique of power. He didn't go in for public executions, the displaying of the head afterwards. He said it was foolish to incite the locals with such tactics.

A tarpaulin was laid out flat on the grass in the square's centre, a guard standing on each of its corners, his rifle slung or leaning against his body. Homemade cigarettes smoked on their lips, between their fingers. The soldiers' uniforms were dirty, dark with sweat and rain and the job of moving the dead from ox-drawn carts into the tents, onto the cots prepared for them. From the square faces of these men, they looked to be of country stock and ill-educated. Seen from under the cover of the command tent, their combined weight preventing the wind from getting underneath the oiled canvas covering and rolling it over, I imagined them muttering obscenities about their orders, how the cots were a waste of precious resources, cussing about Kozu, but mindful of their words regarding Honma, as if the rain itself could pass on their words to the major's ears. These details I remember distinctly Doctor, though in memory, everything seems brighter than it could possibly have been, what with that dark sky and the smell of wet soil. But then again, even lead can be polished to a gloss finish.

When finally I followed Kozu and Honma out from under the cover, my thoughts were on Petrus and what I was finally understanding was certain to become of him -- the four guards would use the tarpaulin, of course, to scoop up Petrus' corpse after the beheading. And yet, with this full knowledge of another's gruesome end, would you begrudge me some selfishness Doctor? For as clear as things were for Petrus, I admit my greatest worries were over our own fearful predicament -- that some unknown power, some circumstance, would prevent Kozu from completing the major's blasted painting of this awful scene and hence, our escape.

The two men strode towards the execution ground, the major's white gloves flashing with a measured rhythm. I could hear only snatches of their conversation, something about standard procedure, how if they were in China the condemned would usually dig a pit for their own remains, before standing over it. Kozu grunted his agreement.

The guards, having disposed of their cigarettes, stood at attention. Honma and Kozu drew near, I close behind. When Petrus was dragged into the open from the other side of the square and delivered onto the tarpaulin, I swear to you Doctor, I could smell his body from where I stood. A tang, like rotten garlic.

'Now, a headstrong type would swipe down with his sword, Yuichiro,' Honma explained with a motion of his hands. 'Doesn't always work. You can miss. I've seen lungs pop out from shoulder cavities and all kinds of things.'

Petrus' eyes were glazed over, his cheek split, the blood sticky. He must have understood what the two officers were discussing, despite the fact he spoke no Japanese. A nod from the major and one of the guards stepped forward and pushed his rifle butt into the back of the Chinaman's knees. Petrus slumped forward, while the guard who had brought him forth stopped his torso from keeling over.

'See how the body sways, Yuichiro; you have to capture that rhythm somehow in my painting. That's how one can miss – if you don't concentrate, if you hesitate. That's why you don't swing your sword like a fool.'

Honma turned to look at the artist.

'Perhaps you would like to do this yourself? What do you say, Yuichiro? Then you could truly step inside the aura of your subject – the ecstasy that follows an execution. Don't you believe it your duty to render such a feeling, to make it sensible? No one else has the power to do so, only you.'

What could have been going through Kozu's head at this point, I can see you are wondering now, as I did then. If Honma had handed you his sword, Doctor, and instructed you to do the act, would you have? What other choice would you have but to kill or to die? Are there any other choices during a time of war? I watched the fingers of Kozu's hand tense.

'This sword I put before you was crafted for such a purpose,' the major said.

In that moment, I thought I saw in Kozu's eyes – not even a flicker, never did he blink -- that he was capable of murder. Not out of fear for his own life as I just put it to you now, but because he was the great Yuichiro

Kozu, a man who would give and take everything for his art.

But I was wrong.

After a pause, Kozu said, 'With respect Major, I must witness the shadow of rapture myself. The wound I can look on afterwards. It is your face I must watch and study.'

Honma nodded and, satisfied, drew his sword. With a curt step, he placed the bevelled edge at the base of Petrus' neck, the hand-guard touching the Chinaman's skin. By the time I had lit one of Trau's cigarettes and drawn the heat of the smoke into my lungs, Petrus' eyes looked out across the grass, hard as marbles, as if searching for something beside Honma's boot.

One at a time, the five other men faced the same fate. The major's gloves remained fantastically white throughout the whole affair.

I should pause here, Doctor, I know, but my story is coming an end.

A strange relief washed over me in the wake of Petrus' execution. *Kozu will surely work quickly now*, I thought; *Honma's portrait is so much smaller in scale and lacking the ambition of his grand tableau for Ambassador Yoshizawa.* The artist, I was sure, would finish soon, like Trau reeling off one of his green vistas. I could almost smell the sea salt, feel the deep sway of the ocean. Having made

the voyage across the South China Sea in the hospital
ship once, I was confident the American's sentimental-
ity would keep us safe. Return we would, and with a
horde of paintings to keep the nation's faith burning.
Your painting, I was certain Doctor, would remain in
Kozu's stead, a gift to the Vietnamese people, a token
that reminded any onlooker where the real threat was
and how easily we had brushed them aside.

I was close to euphoric. And, truth be known, I was
amazed at how quickly I had adjusted to the rigours
of war. How I had not embarrassed myself by vomit-
ing. No one, I believed, had seen me look away at the
last moment – their attention so much drawn to the
Chinaman, to Honma's ancient blade. And what a
bathetic ending the Chinaman had met. He gave no
last words, no valiant gesture of defiance. He simply
knelt, swaying gently from side-to-side. I had somehow expected more at a man's death.

With the major now watching Kozu's every move,
every pencil stroke, the method behind his arrange-
ment of his palette, I was left on the periphery. I
wanted to go back to the villa, to get something to eat,
perhaps to have a cigarette with Trau. The yoke from
his and his sister's neck had been lifted. Petrus' death
meant the villa would conceivably be his. Of course, I
could foresee the military confiscating what rice stocks

Petrus had stored away, and taking over the management of the distillery, but what concern were they of Trau's? He could live out the rest of his days in luxury, his sister beside him and no longer under the heel of the Chinaman.

How was I to return? Believe it or not, I struck out on foot. Without a guard for protection, though, my fear of ambush grew with every corner I took. Every native face appalled me. If I had carried a sword I would have drawn it. The Imperial troops I had seen on the streets after the coup were nowhere to be seen. Black clouds and rain once again stained the air over the Chinese City, like an ink wash, or burning wood.

When I arrived at the front gate of the Yellow House, I looked upon its grandness with nothing but contempt. It was absurd to have such a building in such a country.

At first I thought the place was empty. I called out for the maid with the pox-marked face, but received no answer. But there was a trace of Trau on the air. I could smell solvent, and a deeper pall than turpentine at that. It was bole. As casually as Kozu on that first night in the house, I made my way along the corridor decorated with stencilled vines, to where I knew I would find the wrought iron staircase. Letting my mind wander now that I was safe from the natives outside, I imagined passing down a corridor in one of those root-buried palaces deep in the jungle.

And if you are imagining, Doctor, that Kozu, with one painting on the go, might have finished another, you would be right -- how intuitive you are! When I reached Kozu's studio, I lit the room's candles and I found your painting compete, its soldier's bayonet shining with a lustre beyond oils. In our absence, Trau had taken over from where the master artist had left off. After our summons to bear witness to his brother-in-law's final breath, the young Viet had completed his own portrait, had lifted the painting away from the contingency of the world, not through an inspired choice of green paint, but through gold, rough overlapping shards, smelted and pummelled to a paper-thinness. The texture matched the surface of a worn bayonet well. Only, it was not really Trau's portrait at all. What I saw before me that afternoon was a hero from a distant land. Nonetheless he had done a grand job, having stripped the paint back to the canvas, like a butcher scraping the fat and tissue from a thin bone; and he had not been left alone all that long. How Trau's fingers must have moved with such dexterity; how they must have refused to shake, knowing full well as he did, that he was melding with a masterpiece.

How long I waited on the balcony outside the studio for Trau to return I do not know. The canal was a hive of activity, as was the distillery. It was as if Petrus' death never happened. The incessant call of the insects in the garden, in the nearby paddies, played on my nerves. I may have smoked one of Trau's cigarettes, Doctor, or I may have smoked a couple.

At some point I became aware of the sun and a presence behind me. I turned and found Trau wearing that damned old soldier's uniform. His mouth open, but with no words coming out. He was as white as a ghost. He limped onto the balcony and shrank from the heat of the sun, stopping short after two or three shuffled paces. His clothes were soaked through with sweat. Behind him, to my horror, the young Viet left a slick of blood across the bedroom's floorboards.

'You're not hurt?' I asked, confused, unable to formulate a straight question. My mind drew a blank at the sight of the blood, the boy's pale skin. Trau had been with us during the air raid. I remembered that. He had even made some dry quip about forgetting his matches, when we pulled ourselves from that makeshift grave by the dyke and looked upon the devastation along the canal. I had watched him and Kozu and his sister return to the house to check on Petrus, despite the fact that the place survived with little more damage than some loosened roof tiles.

'Did the Kenpeitai take you? Did they hurt you?'

He shook his head. At that moment, his strength gave out and he fell. I reached down and touched the bloodied rag wrapped around his left foot, unable to believe my own eyes. I prized apart and unwound the layers the material, to find a raw, oozing stump. His big toe was missing.

It would take Trau two days to regain consciousness, waking as he did in the Japanese military hospital near the *Docks de Saigon*. Kozu was with him when he came to. Only then did we find out what had transpired. Trau, Kozu's willing and able apprentice, had taken a chisel and hammer to his own body. To sever the big toe of his left foot at – you'll correct me if I'm wrong, Doctor – what is called the medial joint.

Such a mutilation, Kozu told me while we smoked on the deck of the hospital ship afterwards, was the mark of a thief in the village where he and his sister came from, out in the rice-growing lowlands east of Saigon. With no big toe, a thief could not hope to slink away into obscurity. His identity was forfeit. Everywhere he went afterwards his mark would follow, quite literally, in his footsteps, along every path, between every house, along all the byways that connected one village to another. There he would stand, long after he had walked away, his presence pressed into the red dust like a glyph in a printing press.

'But that does not explain why he did it,' I said.

Kozu tossed his butt into the sea. 'It was the gold leaf.'

The master artist went on to explain to me, how, in order to finish Kozu's portrait the young artist went on the hunt for gold. Without it, the bayonet would be incomplete. The painting's soldier, indeed Trau himself, would not transfigure. So, the young Viet broke into Petrus' bureau, and stole what he needed, believing all the while, Doctor, that his transgression was a crime of little consequence. What was one pair of cufflinks from Petrus' bureau? The man had plenty to spare. Trau broke the gold disks into flakes with the same chisel that would later carve through his flesh and bone, before heating them up, making them soft enough to flatten. The roughness of the process, Doctor, the imperfect finish, the crude application to the canvas: look what they did for that blade. How striking it is.

You are right Doctor. He completed the painting and then the Kenpeitai came for Petrus, while we were engaged at Honma's *green house*. According to

Trau, they arrested the Chinaman in the night, beating him across the thighs with batons when he could not understand what they said. Trau hid with Kieu upstairs, but they were not harassed. His sister never shed a tear. Her quietude horrified him. As such, the young Viet was under no illusion as to why they had come, why they took his brother-in-law away. Petrus, he knew, would disappear.

Sat in his hospital bed, safe under Kozu's protection, Trau confessed to the theft of the cufflinks. Fidelity demanded Trau punish himself. He had stolen from one of his own, from his family, from one of his countrymen. Kozu, of course, dismissed the young Viet's words, the guilt they leaked.

'Art is always worth the sacrifice,' Kozu said.

Doctor, such talk makes me nostalgic for something that should never inspire such a sentiment. Seeing your parcel there, the painting I know is wrapped up within it, I am filled with desire. I cannot give you what you want. But the thought of the Americans taking such a work away – it is unbearable. And surely enough, they will pay you a visit soon, Doctor. Of that I am sure. Botticelli looked to be a thorough man.

It is not much, but I guess, I can make you a reduced offer. It cannot be much, but it is what little I have, perhaps just enough to cover the price of the painting's gold leaf, that precious streak of light, which emblazons your soldier's bayonet. Take the small sum as a token, Doctor, a sign of my good will. What else can I offer you, other than a slice or two of baked mountain yam and one last bowl of millet soup? May I suggest that you do take a little something to eat? Something warm. It is a bitter night out there, after all.